GIVE HIM HELL

HELLHOUND CHAMPIONS
BOOK 3

MACY BLAKE   CASEY DRAKE

Give Him Hell

Copyright © 2019 by Macy Blake and Casey Drake

Cover and symbols designed by A.J. Corza, alexandriacorza.com

Version 3_8.23

For Alex who's been there since the beginning

WELCOME TO THE CHOSEN UNIVERSE

The Chosen Universe is a group of interconnected series set in one universe. There is some overlap to the series, so it's recommended to read the books in order. You can download a FREE reading order guide by going here: https://bit.ly/macyreadingorder

Sweet Nothings: The Chosen One Prequel – When Sam Baker discovers a small child at his backdoor, he learns that a world of magic and shifters exists all around him—including the alpha werewolf he had a one night stand with years before.

The Chosen One Series – The mythical Chosen One is set to return with his eight guardians and correct the magical wrongs done centuries before.

Hellhound Champions Series – As the champions of the fire goddess, the hellhounds have one task: keep the secret of the supernatural world safe.

Magical Mates Series – After the Chosen One returns, magic is in the air, and shifters are finally finding their fated mates...with a little help on the side.

Chosen Champions Series – With the magical realm in chaos, a new set of champions emerges to keep the human world secure.

Cosmo and the King – Cosmo never told any of his friends in the human realm that he ran away on his wedding day, leaving his king at the alter. Now Silenus has to track down Cosmo and convince him that they are meant for each other, even though his stubborn fiancé seems determined to challenge him at every turn.

Christmas Sprites Series – With magic in the human realm on the fritz, four Christmas Sprites find themselves trying to keep the Christmas spirit alive in Mistletoe Falls...and finding love along the way.

If you prefer to read in chronological order, check out the Chosen Universe Box Sets.

NICK

Lightning crashed. Close. Too close. Cool blue light bathed the forest for a split second before blackness swallowed it up again. The fur on his face stood on end. Goosebumps crawled over his arm. He tried to make out a path forward, but he couldn't see any kind of way through. He spun around, trying to find anything familiar, but of course there wasn't anything. He'd never been outside the house, as far as he knew. He hadn't been born there, but he also couldn't remember a time before living there. Wind whipped the heavy rain so it battered him from all sides. Lightning struck a tree off to his left, and he jumped.

"Please," he whimpered as he used one of his long claws to carve a deep notch on one of the trees as he hurried forward. He'd been leaving nicks along his path, hoping they would be enough to lead him back to the house so he could save the others. Jenny's screams still rang in his head. They had taken her to The Room. The one they did all their... experiments in. Her scream cut off abruptly, and they all knew what that meant.

Thunder cracked and the sky lit up again. He pushed ahead through a copse of trees, and spilled out onto a road. He recoiled as *light flooded the area. He crab-walked back into the trees, reaching up to scratch the bark even as he tried to hide himself.*

"Hello? Is someone out there?" a soft voice called out.

He couldn't let them get him. He had to get away, to get the others away from them.

"Are you there? Are you hurt?" she asked. She moved further into the trees, stopping right in front of him.

"No, stay away!" he shouted around the fangs. They'd done something to him, and now he was stuck like this. He couldn't let her see him. It was A Rule. The most important Rule. No one could see them like this.

She sat down on the ground in front of him. She smiled and held out her hand. "It's all right. I can help," she said quietly. "What's your name?"

He shook his head. He couldn't remember it. Mrs. Foote had only ever called him lion. Her helpers just called him kid. That's what they called all of them. Some of the newer kids knew their names. The ones that were there before him didn't. They couldn't remember them. He used all their names, as often as he could, so no one else would forget.

"That's all right. We'll give you a new one, okay?" She looked around and noticed the mark on the tree, following the line to another one a few yards back. "How about Nick for now? At least until you remember?"

Something about her made him feel safe. Someone he could trust. He tentatively reached out and took her hand. It was warm, and somehow dry, even in this downpour. He watched as his claws receded, and he could feel his whiskers retreating.

"How?" he sobbed, collapsing into her arms.

"Shhh, little one. I have you. You're safe now."

NICK CRACKED an eye open and stared at the wall. It was still dark out, but he wouldn't be going back to sleep. Not after the nightmares plaguing him more and more lately. Besides, now that he was up he could go in early to work and pick up another shift before his scheduled route. With a groan, he swung his feet over the edge of the bed as he sat up and rubbed one hand over his face. His fingers came away wet. Crying in his sleep again. Not surprising, given his dreams. Memories. Nightmares. Whatever they were. He could still see their faces. They were so clear in his mind. Almost like a freeze-framed video.

He walked to the kitchen on stiff legs. Yesterday's dishes still sat in the sink, along with a stack of takeout containers. He knew he should clean it up, but he couldn't be bothered. Besides, in his mood, he'd probably just throw everything out and buy new forks. Plastic ones, so he wouldn't have to bother washing. It's not like he was a chef or anything. He didn't really care. Right now, all he cared about was aspirin. And caffeine. Caffeine was necessary. He powered on the coffee maker and got dressed while he waited for it to heat up. Then he filled his travel mug and headed in to work, only glancing at the wall in the corner of his living room.

The ride to the distribution center was quiet. Sure, it was three o'clock in the morning, but still. No post-closing time drunks or after-party stragglers on the road. He parked at the back of the lot and went in.

"Morning, Bill," he called as he punched in.

"Hey, Nick. I'd say you're here early, but it's not really for you, is it?"

"Couldn't sleep. Whatcha got today?"

"Lot of offices downtown. Amazon sprees in the 'burbs. Even the outskirts are heavy today."

Nick studied the zip code map Bill had up on the computer in front of him. "I'll take these," he said, pointing to the routes on the furthest edges of their territories.

"You sure? They'll take you all day."

"I don't mind. Good for clearing the mind, you know?"

"If you say so. At least I don't have to worry about assigning them to Frank or Jesse. You know they'd bitch for days."

Nick laughed along with him, mostly because it was expected. He didn't feel much like laughing today.

"All right. We'll get you loaded up while you go plot your route. We're expecting one more truck this morning, and it's got some packages for you. Not much you can do until it gets here."

Nick shrugged. "I'll go help the guys first. Get it done quicker." He clapped Bill on the shoulder and headed deeper into the warehouse.

"I wish I had ten more of you," Bill called as he walked away.

"No, you don't," Nick muttered.

After last night's dream, he didn't even feel like there should be *one* of him, let alone ten. He got busy getting ready for his day. The route he planned took him along all the smallest country roads he could find. He would be crisscrossing the northern part of the county, scouring every inch he could. Searching, searching, searching....

He was exhausted by the time he got home. He'd managed to pick up two more routes that took him back over the western portions of the county he'd already been to. He sighed as he stripped out of his uniform, dropping his shirt on the floor as he headed to his command center in the corner of his living room.

Maps of surrounding counties covered the walls. He'd drawn grids over them, and each grid was crossed off with a big, red 'X'. Looking over the map on the table in front of him, he realized he'd have to move again soon. Try the next county. He sighed and marked off today's grid and went over Tuesday's again while he was at it. Of course, he'd had no luck. Notes and photos were pinned to the wall next to some grids. Possibilities for him to check again later. Maybe he missed something. Maybe the house was shielded. Maybe....

His phone pinged again, with another message from Mikey. *Call me, bro. Got some big news.* Nick shook his head and pushed it out of his mind for now. He loved his brothers, but he couldn't bear for them to talk to him right now. Not with the dream so fresh in his mind. He stared at the wall, spacing out as he focused. He stared until spots formed in front of his eyes and he realized he'd dozed off, his exhaustion finally catching up with him.

"Where are you?" he mumbled before crawling into bed, not bothering to turn out the light. He was out as soon as his head hit the pillow.

He was dreaming again.

At least he knew it this time.

The screams had died down, leaving them all whimpering in each other's arms. Mrs. Foote and her helpers finished with whatever experiment she'd done and had dumped Jenny in the room. Nick did what he could to comfort her. The wolves were gone, on some sort of mission to steal more kids or something. Mrs. Foote had complained about having more mouths to feed.

One of the younger kids had cuddled up next to him. They did that a lot. Eager for some sort of comfort. He did what he could, even though it wasn't much.

"Look at me. Make sure you use their names, got it? But only in here. Don't let them know it. They can't take everything, as long as you keep your name."

The poor kid. He was so scared. And Jenny was fading fast. One or two more trips, that's all she had left. Nick knew it. He'd seen it before, with the older ones who'd been stuck in the room with him before. He had to get out of there. He had to save them. The others were too young, and Jenny too weak. It was all up to him.

Of course, he had been a kid, too. He just didn't realize it at the time.

In the dream, he could hear the rat-a-tat clacks of Mrs. Foote writing her weekly report on her ancient typewriter. He recalled something about how the magic messed with the electronics, especially after they'd done what they did to them. She couldn't use a computer for a couple days afterward. The radio didn't even work right most days. Everything crackled with static and echoed over the speakers.

Nick wanted to get up, but he was still trapped in the dream-state. Memories choked him as he slept. Things he should remember when he woke up; things that might be important later. He tried to study the house, but all he saw were the dingy, dusty rooms they never left. Sheets yellowed with age, frayed on the edges, piled on the floor with cracked foam mattresses.

"I don't see anything in here," he said as he took in his surroundings. Just then, the radio clicked on, that static that he couldn't forget playing loudly, filling up his mind. "The radio," he whispered. There was that spot, on the road. His radio played fine, and then all of a sudden, it cut out.

Like he drove through a pocket in the world.

"The radio," he repeated, shouting it this time.

Then the world started spinning. He tried to grab on to something, but there was nothing there. The walls disappeared, and the floor changed, the wood floating away, getting replaced with a map. He felt like he was on a globe, being spun as fast as it could. Then suddenly, it stopped. Both his stomach and his mind lurched. His eyes snapped open, wide awake now. He flew out of bed and ran to his desk. He leaned over looking at the map, trying to find that spot again. He was so close. He sniffled and wiped the back of his hand across his nose. It came away bloody. Not surprising, given the vertigo of the dream. A drop of blood fell and hit the map in front of him. Then everything stopped. He barely noticed his own breathing as he took in the bright red against the yellow and blue lines.

There. Right fucking there.

He grabbed his phone and keys and ran toward the door. Maybe he could bribe Bill into letting him off today. He'd put in enough hours this month anyway. The extra shifts helped his finances, and furthered his quest, but the company certainly benefited. Maybe he'd tell him it was some kind of religious holiday. Not that he really practiced any kind of organized religion. Mama Thea told him about the goddesses, and he knew the myth of the Chosen One, but he didn't really follow any of them. If there really were goddesses and champions, surely they would have saved them as kids. He remembered

Mikey's call from the night before, and not for the first time wished he could tell them about his mission. He couldn't, though. His brothers didn't know about the whole supernatural thing. It wasn't his place to let the cat out of the bag, so to speak.

"Cat. Rowr." He laughed, feeling light for the first time in years. Giddy, even. After ten years of searching, he'd finally found it. "We're almost there, Mama Thea. I know where the house is now," Nick whispered as he rubbed his thumb over the charm she'd given him.

It was the first thing she gave him. Well, after giving him a home, that is. The first personal thing that was *his*. It was a simple wooden disk with a lion carved on it. Nothing fancy, but priceless to him. It was powerful. At least it had been to his fourteen-year-old mind. It made him a part of their family. Just like Mikey's pendant that he always wore on a cord around his neck, only his was special for him. Nick didn't wear it anymore, but he did carry it around in his pocket most of the time. He needed the reminder that he was safe more than he cared to admit.

The road took him about thirty miles out of town, to the very edge of the county. He'd been in the area a few times, had been over these same roads in his searches. Nothing but one-lane roads and abandoned barns. Another fifteen minutes and he'd be in the suburbs of the next town over.

His dinosaur of a truck rumbled and shook over the deep ruts along the dirt road that circled around the property. He didn't know how he missed it before, but there it was, looming in the distance. He stopped the truck and stared at it for a while. The outline was just visible in the moonlight. No lights were on in the house, but that wasn't surprising. No one should be up at this hour, even if someone did still live in the house.

How long he sat there, he didn't know. There were so many memories attached to this place. Horrible memories. He wished he'd been able to confide in his brothers so he didn't have to go in there alone. But he couldn't. Thinking of Sawyer and Mikey gave him strength and courage. He was their big brother. They counted on him. Just as the other kids had. He wouldn't let them down again. Finally, he opened the door and stepped out onto the gravel.

"We found it, Mama Thea," he rubbed at the charm again. It warmed up under his fingers. He held the keys in his fist, letting the charm dangle from his hand, his only company in the dim, predawn light as he began to creep forward, his boots crunching on the lumpy gravel drive.

Even from a distance, he could tell no one was there. He just knew it. Hell, he'd known it for a long time now, ever since he took off the charm, really. It wasn't just his imagination: it did have power, even if he didn't really understand how or what or why. None of it. He'd never taken the time to ask the kinds of questions he should have, and then it was too late. The only person who had answers was gone.

Mama Thea had tried to explain it to him when he turned eighteen. The charm muddled his memories of where he'd been, of what had happened here. It also shielded the black magic that still clung to him, keeping him hidden from anyone who might be looking for him. He had been so angry with her, couldn't understand *why* she had arranged to keep it from him. It took a couple of weeks before he was ready to listen to her explanations. Only after he'd felt some kind of ... shift around him that he couldn't completely understand. The air around him was lighter, like he could breathe again.

She assured him she had tried to get back to where she'd found him, but all of his marks were gone. The trees were somehow whole again. His path had been lost. She had enlisted the help of some witches she knew, but their seer could only sense dark forces at work. In the end, all she could do was try to protect him. The charm kept him safe from anyone who may be searching for him and from his own memories.

He got it. Sort of. He'd been fourteen and angry at the world. Scared and out of the house of horrors for the first time in his life. He didn't do well in school, beating himself up for every failure, to the point where he eventually just stopped going. Mama Thea tutored him as best as she could, but he'd been out of control. It made a sort of sense after he found out everything. Less than a month after their talk, he'd started searching. And now he was here, still trying to work up the courage to walk up those steps.

He wanted to go inside the house. *Needed* to, actually. He needed to see it for himself. See if it lived up to the nightmares he still had. He took a deep breath to steel his nerves and took a step forward. Magic fluttered around him and he stopped walking, trying to interpret the strange feelings around him.

Keep out.

The warning only strengthened his resolve. He ignored it and moved forward again.

Another warning buzz from the magic around him, and he realized what he was feeling. Wards. Someone was protecting the house. And that meant they knew he was there. This one was more than a warning. It stung and he clenched his fists and powered through.

They weren't going to stop him. Not now. Not when he was so close to finding answers. Nick bolted up the steps and barreled through the door, shoving it so hard it bounced off the wall and slammed shut behind him. He crashed into the open front room. There was no doubt about it. This was the house. He'd found it!

"Hey! Anyone?" he shouted as he went room to room around the bottom floor. No one was there, and it was just as dusty as it was in his dreams. It was unnaturally quiet. Subconsciously, he could tell no one had lived there for years, maybe even a decade. There was even more dust than the last time he'd been there. There were dishes on the counter. Leftovers from the meager meals they'd been given had dissolved into dust on the plates. He wandered into Mrs. Foote's office. He shivered as he walked through the door. It was one of the rooms they'd never been allowed in. The desk had been cleaned off, and the drawers emptied. A couple were left open, and one had been pulled out and left on the floor, as if whoever cleaned them out couldn't be bothered to right them.

He passed the door leading to the basement, but he couldn't bring himself to even open it, let alone go down there. That was where.... Yeah, he couldn't think about it. Not here. Not without reliving it.

He rushed up the stairs, looking for answers that might tell him what had happened here, where everyone might have gone. Memories crashed over him as he stepped into the bedroom, forcing him to his knees. Bright lights flashed in his eyes and the faces of the other kids floated in his mind as he looked around. He could still smell them there. He remembered a joke Jenny had once told about Mrs. Foote, but he couldn't bring himself to laugh about it. Tears spilled down his face as he reached out to the foam-rubber mattress on the floor. So many nights huddled together, trying their best to comfort each other.

He'd have to wait until morning. The darkness kept him from finding any smaller clues. But he would find something to help him. Anything. He wouldn't stop until he found them.

He heard a noise from outside and ran back downstairs. His body crackled with tension and he glanced down. He had claws for hands and wanted nothing more than to use them. Instead, he held back, looking out the dirty window at the yard.

A ring of fire had appeared between Nick and his truck, and two figures stepped out of it. The first was smaller, and kind of funny looking. He looked like he was wearing furry chaps and a helmet of all things. The other guy had Nick worried. He was huge, his eyes burned a fiery red, and his body was ... steaming? His blond mohawk was combed back into a ponytail at the back of his head. The braids in his beard reminded Nick of a Viking.

He turned around and braced himself, prepared to fight. He was ready for it. It was time. He opened the front door, drawing the attention of the two new arrivals.

"Who are you?" the giant Viking demanded. "What business do you have here?"

Nick's skin prickled, anger like he'd never felt before coursing through him. "I don't want to kill you, but I will if you had anything to do with this!"

The Viking's eyes dimmed, the fiery red glow fading. "Do with this? Of course we did. What do you think we are?"

"Then prepare to die," Nick growled. He finally had one of the bastards in his hands, and he was ready to exact justice.

JEDREK

Jedrek rolled his shoulders, giving his head a shake to chase away the exhaustion creeping up on him. He couldn't rest. Not yet. His pack, his family was still in danger and they were surrounded by strangers. No, he wouldn't rest and neither would the rest of them. They would do their duty and serve both their goddess and alpha well.

Solomon had gone to see the goddess, hoping to get some information for them on the newest attack. The Chosen One and his guardians had arrived, also injured from an attack. The amount of coordination involved scared Jedrek more than he cared to admit. He wasn't alone.

"I don't understand," Calli grumbled quietly beside him. They continued walking the perimeter, sticking close to the wards.

"Nothing makes sense," Jedrek added.

"If the Chosen One has guardians, why can they not keep him safe?"

Jedrek wondered the same thing. "There are forces at work here that are beyond our abilities."

Calli shivered. "First the aswangs, now this. When is Meshaq coming back? Or Solomon?"

She knew he didn't have the answer, so Jed didn't bother pretending to know. He glanced over the gathered group once more, taking in all of the loners and outcasts. The Jerrick pack had been kind enough to open their home to them all. The young ones were all shaken, Ben especially.

It was the safest place Jed knew of, outside of the Chosen One's home. And yet, even that had been breached. The wards weren't effective against whatever invisible opponent they faced. The air trembled around them and a portal opened. Every pack member prepared for the worst, but they settled moments later when Meshaq, Drew, and Solomon walked through together.

Calli laughed and Jedrek couldn't help smiling also. They had a stack of bakery boxes in their arms, and Drew had a very smug smile on his face. Their alpha's mate had convinced Shaq and Solomon to get doughnuts. He had their entire pack wrapped around his fingers and he knew it. Luckily, he used his powers for baked goods and not evil.

Jedrek and the rest of the pack gathered around. Solomon handed Calli the stack of boxes he held, only holding one back. Of course, he'd have to make sure he took care of Cody, who was still sleeping. The only good thing to come of all of this was that both their alpha and his second in command had found their mates. It shouldn't have been possible, especially considering that Drew was an omega, and yet... they were the bright spots of hope in all of the fear and confusion. Before he could hear their explanation, though, the sigil on Jedrek's arm began to burn.

"Really? I don't even get a doughnut?" Jedrek complained.

"It's the old farmhouse. Where we found the kids," Sol said. "Another coincidence?"

"Probably another hiker," Calli said. She stuffed a jelly doughnut in her mouth and Jedrek scowled her way. Then he turned back to Solomon, confused as to how he knew the details of the sigil. Only

Meshaq, their alpha, was able to know what challenges they might face during their mission. How was Solomon able to...?

"Go, Jed. Let me know if you need me, okay?" Solomon added.

An energy he'd only felt from Meshaq before rolled through him. Something had definitely happened while they were with the goddess.

"Yes, alpha," Jedrek said, finally understanding the change that had occurred during their absence.

Solomon met his gaze and his eyes flared with the flames of their beasts. Jedrek's flashed in return, before he turned and opened the portal, unable to delay any further. The goddess needed him to do something, and even though he wanted nothing more than to stay behind and find out what had happened, how their pack now had another alpha, he couldn't wait.

"Champion, wait."

Jedrek turned and found Cosmo by his side. "You'll have to speak to the others. I have to go."

"I will accompany you."

Jedrek paused at the portal. "Not your job, Cosmo. Stay here and make merry with the others."

Cosmo scowled. "I heard Solomon say you were going to the old farmhouse. You shouldn't go alone."

Before he could stop him, Cosmo skipped through the portal. Jedrek growled and followed him.

"Cosmo," Jedrek protested. "Get back."

"Whatever is happening is not over. We cannot risk losing any of our champions. You need someone to have your back."

Jedrek took a moment to really look at Cosmo. He still held an arm across his stomach, even though he didn't have to hold his guts in anymore. There was a fresh, pink stripe across his lower abdomen, just above his furry hipline. But his jaw was set in a stubborn jut. And he could handle himself. That move he put on the aswang, spearing it with a horn and flipping it over? Bad. Ass.

"Are you even healed?"

"Ready enough for whatever battle lies ahead of us."

"You do realize my goddess would never send me alone if backup were required."

Cosmo huffed and looked around the clearing.

"Seriously, Cosmo, go back to the others. It's fine."

"The children still have nightmares about this place, ten years later," Cosmo said quietly. "Ollie confessed his secret to me not long ago."

It didn't surprise him. The things they'd learned about this place after they rescued the Jerrick kids were horrifying. Add to it the fact that they'd never found the magic users responsible, and he couldn't blame the kids for continuing to fear the place.

Jedrek groaned while taking a glance around. A beat up old truck sat in the driveway, and his senses told him someone was inside the house. Probably looking for a vintage bathtub to steal or something equally idiotic. He caught movement in the front window, and then the door burst open, flying off its hinges and laying on the floor in a cloud of dust and splintered wood. A man stood in the doorway, his breath heaving. Something about him seemed familiar, but not. Jedrek's senses were confused, which rarely happened. The man was some sort of shifter, though, and it immediately put Jedrek on alert.

"Who are you?" Jedrek demanded. "What business do you have here?"

The man partially shifted, and he seemed barely in control.

"I don't want to kill you, but I will if you had anything to do with this!"

Did this idiot think the hellhounds weren't responsible for the wards on this place? Could he not feel their presence?

"Do with this? Of course we did. What do you think we are?"

"Then prepare to die."

It actually took Jedrek a second to process. His exhaustion had clearly given him some sort of brain fog, because this guy had not just threatened to—

"Malfeasant!" Cosmo shrieked as he charged toward the man,

driving him to the ground in an impressive move. He really needed to remember to tell Shaq about Cosmo's skill in battle. He wondered if his alpha— his other alpha now that he had two— would think about it.

The grass in the yard was severely overgrown and shielded most of them from Jedrek's view, but he could see Cosmo's horns when he bobbed his head up and down as he tried his best to whale on the guy. Jedrek sighed and squashed the urge to send Cosmo off to the top of some mountain in the middle of nowhere.

"Okay, killer. Bring it in," Jedrek said as he grabbed Cosmo by the horns to pull him off the man.

"We must kill the interloper!" Cosmo squawked as he squirmed in Jedrek's hands, continuing to kick and scream in some grandiose plan to exact retribution on the trespasser.

"Cosmo. Enough," Jedrek grunted when one of flailing hooves smacked him in the leg.

The stranger smelled like some kind of shifter, but it was off, like the magic that surrounded the *notwolves* they tangled with at this very house. Jedrek had never smelled anything like it, and hadn't since. Hadn't *felt* anything like it either. But this was different. And ... enticing? Jedrek shook his head. *Where the fuck did that thought come from?*

He took a moment to consider him. Judging by his long legs and arms, he'd be nearly as tall as him when he stood. His longish hair spread out wildly around his head like some kind of mane. Honestly, he was beautiful. Jedrek *wanted*. That was what threw him the most. He'd never felt the ache he felt now. The need to just pull someone close and shut the world away for a while. But the faun wriggling in his grip reminded him of the task at hand. *Interrogate now, process it later.*

Jedrek pulled himself to his full height and allowed his eyes to burn bright. His skin heated up in the early morning sun as the power of the goddess flowed through him. "Who are you?" Jedrek demanded. "What business do you have here?"

"Get out of my way," the shifter snapped as he defiantly pushed himself up on his knees. Something was definitely wrong with this guy. "I don't want to kill you, but I will if you had anything to do with this!"

The crazy beautiful stranger was clearly insane along with his more obvious physical problems. "You need to get out of here. This place is none of your concern," Jedrek snarled.

He only had time to toss Cosmo aside before the shifter sprung, swiping at him with his claws. He wasn't steady on his feet, and something was very wrong with his change. He seemed stuck, trapped in an inbetween. Half man, half lion, but neither side of him fully in control. Jedrek had no idea what to do, but he managed to get a grip around the shifter's neck.

"Get him Jedrek! He hurt Henry and the others!" Cosmo's cheer enraged the shifter further, and he swiped at Jedrek with his claws.

"Cosmo—"

But Cosmo wasn't in any mood to listen.

"That does it." Cosmo stamped his feet and huffed loudly as he geared up to attack the man again. Jedrek let him get two steps in before he opened a portal between them and Cosmo ran into it, sending him back to the Jerrick's place. Hopefully he wouldn't take out any tents as he ran through the clearing or trample any of the refugees. Of course, his distraction meant that the shifter managed to jerk free. The man roared in his face before running back into the house. Jedrek could just make out what he was saying.

"I have to save them. It's been too long. I need to help them," he kept repeating as he smashed into the door full-force, splintering it as it slammed open.

This...creature...had fought him. Bravely, if stupidly. Jedrek stood there, half-shifted, in all his fiery hellhound glory, and this sort of half-shifter, who smelled *amazing*, was not stepping down. He had roared back at him, of all things. Jedrek had never seen that. Usually when a hellhound showed up, the person knew they were in deep shit. Most times, there were tears. Groveling was normally involved, along with a lot of snot and pissing of pants. Either that, or he was faced with an evil he had to immediately put down or deliver to the gates for the goddess to pass judgment.

This. This was something else. Something different. And the shifter had turned his back on Jedrek, not to run away. But to run back into the house of horrors. It took Jedrek a moment longer to make the only connection he had left: he must have lived there, as a child. Or, more accurately, he'd been kept there, having his magic tampered with, just like the others. No wonder he smelled faintly of the bad magic they'd found ten years ago. It must have clung to him, preventing his full shift, and marking him with dark witchcraft. That was the familiar smell. He'd been surrounded by it for so long, from Ben and the others, that he hadn't made the connection. But this shifter had another layer of magic on him as well. Who was he, and where had he come from?

Ben had told them about others, kids who lived there before, ones that hadn't made it. Only this one *got away.* Somehow, he managed to get out of the nightmarish house and survive. Jedrek didn't understand how that was possible. How had he stayed hidden for so long? Meshaq had an entire network of shifters and magic users scouring the world for any traces of the sorcery they'd encountered, yet this shifter came to them, stumbling across their wards on his own.

He let the shifter go on ahead. He could hear him running from room to room, shouting as he went. No one answered, and he was becoming more frantic as he pounded up the stairs. They'd all been gone for more than ten years, but there was no way this shifter could have known that. He couldn't imagine what he must be going through, being back here. Willingly going into that nightmare factory, even after so many years, couldn't be easy. Yet, he didn't give it a second thought before he crashed through the door.

He considered calling in reinforcements, but decided against it. If this man really was who Jedrek thought he might be, the roller coaster of emotions could trigger an all-out war. As it was, he was probably in for a fight on his own. The sobs he heard from the house tugged at his heart and took him back to those early days after they'd rescued Ben, Henry, and the others. They'd been broken, too, but Sam and Vaughn had carefully helped them come to terms with their past and build a future as a family.

This man clearly hadn't had that opportunity. But it didn't mean Jedrek could just let him go on a tear through the house. They kept the wards around the place for a reason.

"No time like the present," Jedrek mumbled to himself as he decided it was time to intervene. He made sure to make noise as he climbed the stairs and stepped up onto the porch. Sneaking up on a shifter in distress was idiotic, even if he was pretty sure he could take him. He carefully stepped over the remnants of the door and quickly surveyed the damage. He only made it two steps before he had a partially shifted— lion? Jedrek wasn't sure. The guy's magic was really screwed up—flying at him, claws out and ready for battle. He blocked the swipe and caught him in mid-air before shoving him against the wall.

"Where is he?" the shifter shouted frantically.

"Who?"

"You know who! Where is he?" He thrashed in Jedrek's arms, fighting back almost hard enough to dislodge himself until Jedrek had to set him back on the floor or risk seriously harming him. "Where are they? What did you do to them?"

"Now just hold on. I think we need to talk." Jedrek held his hands up in front of himself to try to placate him.

"Why? So I can listen to your lies? I'm not listening anymore." His words were slightly slurred because of the fangs. He pounced again, obviously intending to slash Jedrek's throat, leaving Jedrek no choice but to defend himself.

"Sorry," Jedrek whispered as he slammed his fist into the side of the shifter's head. He went down like a ton of bricks. This close, Jedrek could tell he was definitely a lion shifter, and a powerful one at that, but his shift was definitely fucked up in a major way. The power coming from the guy was immense, though. Probably an alpha, which just made him that much more dangerous if he was out of control.

He checked the lion's pockets and found his wallet. Nick Smith, the ID said. "Nice to meet you, Nick." The address was about forty-five minutes away. "Goddess, kid. Who the hell are you?"

He debated taking the truck, but he opened a portal instead, aiming for the apartment. He wanted to get him as comfortable as he could as quickly as possible. Anyone who'd been through what happened at this house deserved his respect.

He picked Nick up and carried him bridal style and stepped through the portal into a darkened one-room apartment. He quickly laid Nick on the bed. Then he checked the freezer for ice but only found a bag of corn and a tub of cherry ice cream. He grabbed the corn and went back to the bed. It would be better than nothing. Anything to help keep the swelling down. He didn't mean to hit him quite so hard, but between the threat Nick posed and his momentum as he flew toward him, he hit him harder than he planned to. He laid the corn across Nick's forehead and left him to rest. While he waited, he took a look around. There wasn't a lot to it. One-room studio apartments didn't lend themselves to privacy. Living area, kitchen with a square card table standing off to one side, and a bedroom nook.

The living area was set up more like a command center than for any kind of comfortable entertaining. Maps and charts lined the walls, and two folding tables were pushed up against each other, covered with more maps. There was a drop of blood on the map on the table, marking the spot where they had just been.

"Goddess," Jedrek mumbled. He glanced at the notes pinned to the wall, stopping at an old newspaper clipping. The headline told of a car accident taking two lives. He perused the article, stopping and gasping at the words. The couple had been survived by their three children: Nick, Michael, and Sawyer Smith. He took a step back and stared at Nick where he lay unconscious across the room.

He was the Chosen One's *brother*?

Jedrek turned back to the wall, taking in the years of notes and the meticulous method Nick had used to search. It was impressive, even more so that he'd actually found the place at all. They'd kept it locked down so tightly that only a magic user should have been able to pick up on it. They couldn't really prevent the random hiker from showing up, but they had been able to make it nearly impossible to find the house unless someone knew what they were searching for.

Of course, as the Chosen One's brother, it didn't really surprise Jedrek that Nick had been able to find the house. It opened up a whole other realm of questions, though. Jedrek would definitely have to get some answers from Nick the moment he woke up.

Jedrek couldn't help but smirk at his next thought, though. Cosmo was going to shit bricks when he figured out just who it was he'd tried to kill, and Jedrek couldn't wait to see his reaction. It would have to wait, because Nick was starting to wake up.

NICK

A throbbing ache woke Nick and he debated the wisdom of opening his eyes. But then something cool dripped on his face. He sure as shit didn't put it there. He felt like he'd been run over by a Mack truck. Had he finished his shift? Goddess, it hurt to think.

Wait. He'd been...

He sat up quickly, immediately regretting it, and a bag of frozen corn fell onto his lap. His head spun and his stomach lurched, but he managed to force it down. He groaned as he recognized where he was. His own bed. Had it all been one of his infamous nightmares? No, it couldn't have been.

"No. No, no, no. What am I doing here? I need to save them." He stood up and stumbled toward the door.

"Nick. Stop."

The Viking from the house was there. In his place. It had been real. *It had been real.* He'd finally found it. But they were back at his apartment? His head throbbed and he resisted the urge to put the corn back onto it. He had no idea what had happened or how he'd managed to get back home.

"What the hell?"

"Close," the Viking said, smirking. His eyes glowed orange, and Nick took a step back. "Please, sit down. We need to talk."

Nick gulped and nodded as he sat back down on the bed. It wasn't like he had that much furniture anyway, and this...whatever he was stood between him and the only chair in the room. "You, uh. You know my name."

"Yes. Sorry. I found your identification in your wallet. My name is Jedrek." He held a hand over his chest and gave his head a slight bob as he introduced himself.

Memories came back. He'd gone through the house. He'd attacked this guy. He'd...

"You knocked me out."

"Yes. You seemed intent on destroying me, and I couldn't let that happen."

He'd been out of his mind, and yeah, he'd pretty much wanted to do some damage to this guy and the little furry one, who was nowhere to be seen. His nerves were shot, something crawling beneath his skin demanding he defend himself. Get answers. Find the others.

"Sorry, but I need to move." Nick stood on wobbly legs and started to pace around the room. Too much had happened, and he needed to work it out in his mind. In all the years of searching, he'd never imagined what he'd actually do when he found the house. He'd definitely never imagined finding a giant of a man with flaming eyes who, on second thought, seemed to be keeping an eye on the place. Which reminded him. "How did we get here? We were *there*." He shivered as he said it. He glanced out the window and noticed it was light out, but he had no clue what time it was. Last he remembered they were in the dim hours of pre-dawn. *How long ago was that?*

"I brought you back here when you passed out."

"When you knocked the shit out of me, you mean."

Jedrek shrugged at his response. "What were you doing there?"

"I could ask you the same thing."

They stared at each other, each waiting for the other to offer up an explanation. Nick would be damned if he caved first. He had no clue who this guy was, or if he could be trusted.

Jedrek uncrossed his arms and waved one toward Nick's research wall. "I need an explanation."

And he clearly wasn't going to tell Nick a thing until he got one. Nick clenched his jaw, fighting the urge to go into attack mode again. For the first time in a decade, he had someone with information. He couldn't lose this chance because he had a sneaking suspicion he wouldn't get another one. Nick sighed. "Fine. I've been looking for that house for a while."

"How long?"

"Does it matter? No one was there anyway."

"I know," Jedrek replied.

"How did you know? Did you kill them?" Nick's lip curled in a snarl, his out of control emotions getting the best of him once again.

"No," Jedrek said quietly. "We would never hurt cubs. No matter what. We saved them."

It took a second for Jedrek's words to sink in, but when they did, Nick's legs went weak. "Saved? When? Who?"

"It was around ten years ago now," Jedrek replied gently.

Nick's legs did buckle under the implications, and he landed hard on his knees. "Ten years... the whole time... they were already... the whole fucking time."

He shook his head and stared at the floor. He jumped when he felt a hand on his shoulder after a moment. Jedrek had moved across the room without making a sound.

"I'm sorry," Jedrek said. "I can tell you have been searching for a long time."

"How?" Nick rumbled, his mind filling with questions.

"The little one managed to get away and find help. They have lived with an alpha we trust since then."

"Little one? How many were there?"

"There were six when we found them."

"*Six.* Holy shit. If I had only..."

He couldn't finish the thought. His emotions were choking him and robbing him of his words. The hand on his shoulder squeezed tighter.

"How long were you there?"

"I don't know."

"How did you get away?"

"I can't remember."

"Okay. How long ago was it?"

"Fourteen years," Nick whispered. The tears he'd been holding at bay finally started falling freely.

"Oh, Goddess," Jedrek murmured.

"My memories were blocked for a long time." He reached into his pocket and tugged free his keys. "This... it kept them from me."

Jedrek glanced at the charm and his eyes widened before he turned back to look at Nick.

"What is it?" Jedrek asked.

"I don't know," Nick confessed. "It muted the memories for so long. Protected me from...what, I don't know. Until Mama told me it was time to take it off. Mikey has one too."

"Do you know where she got them?"

Nick shook his head. "A friend of hers made them. I was so angry at the time. If I had been able to get back there, I might have been able to help."

"I don't think it would have worked out that way. They would have been after you. You, getting away, that would have been disastrous for their plans. It protected you. That charm, it must have been blessed. By the mother goddess herself. And she blessed you with it. That charm is the proof of it."

The charm warmed again, the second time it had done it. Nick held it tightly and wished he had more answers.

Jedrek gave his shoulder another squeeze, and Nick was oddly comforted by the gesture. He felt the same unfamiliar urge from earlier, and his hands began to transform.

"What's wrong with me?"

"I don't know."

"I haven't... the charm, I think it kept me from shifting, too. I haven't shifted since... that night. The night I got away."

Jedrek made a weird grunting sound and his thumb began to stroke over Nick's collar bone. He wanted to turn his neck to the side, allow more room, but the urge seemed wrong, somehow. He grit his teeth instead and focused on other details.

"It's been a weird night. I felt the first ward, but it took me a minute to figure out what it was. The second one kind of pulled at my lion." He chuckled. "It felt so damn weird. It's been so long."

"Wait a minute. Second ward? And it pulled your lion out?"

"Yeah. You mean you didn't know about it?"

Jedrek shook his head. "No. We only placed an outer ward to notify us of trespassers. I don't know of any other wards on the place. Did it do anything else?"

"Not that I can remember. I stopped in front of the house, and then when I took a step forward, something pulled at me. Next thing I knew, I had claws again and my senses were out of sorts. A few more steps, and I felt another tingling."

"You never shifted. In fourteen *years*."

"No," Nick snarled. He pulled away, suddenly annoyed by the interrogation. He pushed to his feet and went into the kitchen, but he was only frustrated by the mess and the smell of old food. He snarled again, but this time it came out lower, more gravely. More like a lion. "Not all the way. I was stuck in a half-kind of shift for years before Mama Thea found me, but she helped me shift back. Then, nothing. Not until tonight."

"I'm sorry," Jedrek said gently. "I'm just trying to get as much information as possible. We would never have placed any wards to force a shift."

"We?" Nick asked. His voice still low and not his own. His skin itched and he started to scratch his arm before remembering that his hands were clawed.

Jedrek's eyes changed again, the same flames from earlier reappearing and the itch eased, fading into the background. "How much do you know of our world?"

Nick shrugged. Not enough, that was for sure. But he didn't want to confess his ignorance. He wished, not for the first time, that he'd insisted Mama Thea tell him what she knew instead of sticking his head in the sand and pretending it all wasn't real.

"I am a hellhound. My pack and I are tasked with protecting the human realm and defending the secrets of the supernatural world. We are the champions of the fire goddess."

Nick was almost one hundred percent sure he was blinking like an idiot, but what did you say to a guy saying he works for a goddess. Not much, that's what you say. "Okay?"

Jedrek sighed. "I know. I have a lot to explain to you, but I need to make sure you're in control of your shift."

"I don't think I am," Nick said. His voice felt growly again, lower than it should be. He instinctively tightened his hold on his charm once more, and it warmed beneath his touch.

"Can you try to shift?"

"I don't know." Truth was, Nick was scared to try. It had been so long, he'd learned to live without it. He didn't even know how he managed to shift back to human at the house.

"Could you try it? I'd like to check your form, make sure there are no lingering effects."

"Lingering affects? Like what?"

"Traces of magic, or mutations—"

"*Mutations*? You think they Frankenshifted me?" Nick was trying really hard not to panic.

"No. That's not it."

Nick narrowed his eyes. "That's exactly it, isn't it? They've done it before, haven't they?"

"Calm down," Jedrek said. "We don't know what they may or may not have done. The others, they could still shift, but they don't have partial shifts like you do. It's okay if you can't, Nick. We'll see what we can do to help you."

"Fuck. Okay. I'll try."

Honestly, Nick kind of wanted to shift again, just to feel it. He'd felt so powerful when he'd been partially shifted earlier, like nothing could stop him. But he didn't know if he could, and he didn't want to make a fool of himself in front of Jedrek. Or anyone. He'd like to be alone to fail at the one thing that should be instinctual to him.

"Give me a second," Nick added.

"Um..."

Nick looked up. "What?"

"You should probably take your clothes off first."

Nick could feel himself blushing. He had nothing to be ashamed of, body-wise, but his ignorance had always been a sore spot for him. He hated not knowing things, even though he struggled with learning and had ever since he'd left the house having no education at all.

But Jedrek wasn't looking at him like he was stupid. He looked like he understood, somehow, that Nick was out of practice. That he'd forgotten more than he ever knew about how to be a lion.

He moved to the center of the room and stripped off his clothes before closing his eyes. He took a couple of breaths to center himself, and then pictured himself as a lion. He conjured up every image of lions he could think of. It took a few minutes, but he finally felt that tingle again. His skin crawled and his muscles shifted. The bones realigned themselves, and then he was a lion. Simple as that. He shook out his mane and then turned to look at Jedrek.

Jedrek looked impressed. A flutter of pride moved through Nick and he shook his mane once more before striding forward. His feet didn't feel like his own. His legs trembled and he wasn't quite sure how to move on four legs instead of two. But he moved forward and bumped his head against Jedrek's side.

"Wow," Jedrek whispered. "You're breathtaking."

Nick bumped his head against Jedrek again, wanting him down, lower to the ground. He wanted to scent him, to cover him. He pushed harder, but Jedrek grabbed a handful of his mane and pulled his head up. His eyes flared, flames engulfing them.

"Control yourself."

Nick snarled and bumped him once more. He was the predator here, not this man. He was in control. He was stronger, more powerful. A hunter. He pushed against the man once more then reared up on this hind legs to use his front paws to batter at him.

The man was strong. He didn't go down. Nick snarled and it turned into a displeased roar. He demanded submission and this man would give it to him.

"Nick!"

The man gave him a shove, and Nick fell back. He rolled away before clumsily trying to regain his feet. He turned and prepared to roar once more, but the man was gone. And in his place stood a large, black beast with flames for eyes. It roared at him and Nick trembled, for once uncertain. He was the predator. Wasn't he?

He blinked and human thoughts began to come back. A rumbling whine escaped his throat and he sat down. The beast huffed and a puff of steam escaped his lips. A moment later, he was human again. Nick grumbled, but it came out as another displeased roar.

"You're going to be a giant pain in my ass, aren't you?" Jedrek said. "You've got to get yourself under control, Nick. Fight for it. Think. Use your human side."

He didn't want to. He liked this version of himself. His senses were telling him everything he needed to know. He didn't need to think of anything else. He wanted. And he was hungry. And he needed to piss. And he was hungry. Nick snarled, demanding his needs be met. He wanted, and this human would get what he wanted for him.

But he wasn't human. He was something else. Something strong and powerful on his own. But Nick *wanted*.

Nick snarled again, his frustration building.

"Come on, Nick. *Think*."

JEDREK

Under normal circumstances, Jedrek would have a completely different reaction to a shifter challenging his authority the way Nick currently was. But he'd also seen how difficult the shift was for him, and knowing that he'd not shifted in so many years made Jedrek more forgiving than he would be otherwise.

"Come on, Nick."

Behind the lion's eyes, a predator stared back at Jedrek waiting for the moment to pounce and judging his worthiness as a competitor. Jedrek had been a hellhound for a lot of years, and he knew when he was being sized up. Nick wanted to take him down and prove his dominance.

And Jedrek had exactly zero plans for letting that happen.

He'd at least gotten Nick to back away a little, but the danger was still there. Jedrek had taken down bigger, more experienced shifters before, even a few with alpha blood flowing through their veins like Nick clearly had. He could feel the power rolling off of him, pent up for way too long to be safe. Jedrek wanted to get him back in control, mostly because he really needed to let Nick know that his brothers were hurt. But he had to get him stabilized first. No way was he planning to take him to the compound in this state. He had no control over his shift, and that meant he wasn't going anywhere near the others.

"Nick, I need you to shift back now. Come on. Show me you can do it."

The lion snarled, baring his teeth at Jedrek. He didn't pounce, though, but Jedrek could see the plan forming behind his eyes. Then he spotted the charm on the floor by Nick's clothes. Nick's muscles flexed and Jedrek leapt, diving to the side and scooping up the charm at the same moment he was hit by several hundred pounds of lion. He rolled, using his experience and training to regain the upper hand before pressing the charm into Nick's fur.

He didn't expect the burning. He really didn't expect the damn thing to explode in his hand. Nick yowled in pain and Jedrek couldn't help his own hiss. Both of them were marked, and Jedrek's hand was red and mottled where the charm had singed him. But the move had served its purpose: after a moment, clarity returned to Nick's eyes.

"You back with me?"

Another snarl, but this one more human sounding, as if Nick wanted an explanation for what was going on. Jedrek wished he had one as well. He'd had to curb his reactions when listening to Nick's story. He wanted to hunt down the magic users responsible and bring them to the goddess for judgment. But he'd wanted the same thing for over a decade with no results. It was the only time in his pack's existence that they'd failed. The magic users who'd hurt these cubs— and who knew how many more— had disappeared.

Nick made another noise, this one curious. He wanted to know what Jedrek was thinking. Instead of answering, he ran his hand over Nick's mane and met his warm brown eyes. "You ready to shift back yet?"

Another rumbling sound but then Nick moved and knocked Jedrek backward once more. Before he could protest, Nick plopped down on top of him and thumped his large head down on Jedrek's chest.

"You're really not a house cat, you know?"

Nick didn't seem to care. Jedrek couldn't imagine how his instincts must be reacting to the presence of a hellhound. But somehow, Nick must have figured out that Jedrek really wasn't out to hurt him. And that... that was pretty spectacular, considering the circumstances. Of course, if anyone in his pack saw him in his current predicament, he'd never live it down.

He gave in and ran his hand over Nick's mane once more, settling in for what amounted to a cuddling session with a full grown lion. Nick's size rivaled Jedrek's hellhound form, barely a head shorter overall. His body held tightly-controlled power and his mane framed his expressive face. Human thought had begun to creep back into his eyes, but the lion side of Nick was still very much in control. The beast was so proud that he'd managed to get Jedrek under his control.

And Jedrek let him have the moment of pride. They both knew deep down that Jedrek could reverse the situation in a moment. Nick butted his head against Jedrek's hand and flicked an ear.

"Oh, you want me to pet you now, huh?"

Teeth bared.

"Don't get snarly with me. And move your arm. You're going to dislocate a rib. You weigh a ton."

Snarl.

"You want me to move?"

Nick grumbled but moved slightly to the side, taking some of his weight from Jedrek's chest.

"That's better."

Jedrek took a chance and ran his hand over Nick's side. The muscles twitched under his hand, but he didn't move away or make another angry snarl.

"It's okay, Nick," Jedrek said softly. "It can be an adjustment."

Nick snorted and he gave Jedrek a look that clearly said he was a master of the obvious.

Jedrek grinned. "That first shift is a doozy. But you're doing great. You just need to think about being human again. The lion's a bit possessive, right? He's in charge right now, but you're in charge, too. It's a partnership. I need you to be human again, though. So let him know it's okay, and that you won't have to wait so long to shift again. I can help with that."

Jedrek could see the understanding in the lion's eyes, so he knew Nick could hear him, but it didn't seem to be making a difference. Nick wasn't making an effort to shift back at all, but at least he seemed to be processing the request. Human emotions were in the lion's eyes as well. Fear, confusion, anger, all blurring together. And even a little happiness, probably at being back in his fully shifted form. His instincts had to be battering at him.

"Just relax and breathe," Jedrek said quietly. "Think about being yourself, and you'll change back." Nick whined and Jedrek chuckled. "Yeah, I get it. You want to stay this way. It's tempting, but you've unlocked it now, Nick. You'll be able to shift again. I'll help you. And if I can't, I know a ton of people who can. But now I need you to deal with this and shift back. We've got some stuff to talk about and I need to actually hear you and not interpret your growls and snarls."

Nick huffed and pushed himself up. He tottered around on his four paws and tried to get his balance. He staggered a bit and tripped over his own feet before he got the hang of it. Then his tail swished and knocked a glass of the table. The clatter startled him and he let out a roar that would probably scare every neighbor in a five block radius. But there wasn't anyone around. Jedrek had already listened to make sure there weren't any unsuspecting humans who would be initiated into their world if they saw or heard something suspicious. He was, first and foremost, a hellhound, and Jedrek knew his duty to the secret well.

Jedrek couldn't help but grin at Nick's raised hair hissing at the broken glass though. Of course, Nick noticed and turned to snarl at him. Jedrek shook his head and held his hands up in surrender. "It's okay, man." Nick advanced on him, backing him into the counter, growling lowly the whole time. "Seriously, dude. We're cool."

But the broken glass had been worse for Nick's control than

Jedrek realized. The growling grew more insistent, demanding submission once more, and Jedrek's hackles couldn't help but rise at the challenge. When Nick lowered to the ground like he was planning on pouncing, Jedrek didn't stop the shift from taking over. His hellhound form was huge, standing tall over Nick. He huffed at the lion when he came close.

Nick didn't try to attack, thank goddess, but he didn't exactly back down from the provocation. He lowered his head and nudged Nick's shoulder and was impressed when Nick didn't even budge. Instead, he shoved back, and Jedrek was forced to step back to rebalance himself.

Everything was so much simpler in his hellhound form. Some things were sharper—sight, smell, hearing. Colors were muted, and tinted orange by the flare of his eyes. But even as an animal, he was still himself, able to understand at least the basics of most things happening around him, but the emotions were dulled. Or limited, maybe. Simple, basic emotions—fear, safety, happiness, those things came through. But there was no room for jealousy, shame, and doubt.

Most importantly for Nick, animals didn't carry the kind of overwhelming confusion that had been crushing him even a few minutes earlier. He circled around Nick, and Nick's scent hit Jedrek hard. Something about him made Jedrek want to rub against him and transfer his own scent deep into Nick's fur. He gave in to his instincts and rubbed his side against Nick's again.

Nick curled a lip in a silent warning, but he let out a little purr as he brushed his face into Jedrek's shoulder. He let out a little yip when he felt Nick's jaws gently close on the side of his neck. The moment was intense. He'd never let anyone near his neck, yet he couldn't think of anything he wanted more in that moment.

Before he could follow that thought any further, he heard the telltale crackling in the air that signaled the arrival of one of his kind. A moment later, Solomon stepped through a portal and into the small apartment. Jedrek had a second to register the shock on Sol's face before he shifted back into his human shape, hurrying to form an explanation for his new alpha.

"Sol—"

But Solomon wasn't there for an explanation.

"We'll talk about this later. I'm looking for Sawyer's brother, Nick."

Jedrek glanced at the lion snarling in annoyance at his side. He grabbed Nick by the mane once more, hoping he understood that Solomon was not to be challenged.

Of course, it wasn't going to work out that way. Nick roared, and Jedrek winced.

"Shit," Jedrek grumbled as Solomon turned his flaming stare onto the lion. Within seconds, Solomon transformed into his hellhound form, and then he let out a roar of his own. Jedrek dropped to his knees and bared his neck. And that didn't impress Nick either. He fought the powerful urge, teeth bared and the hair of his mane standing on end. But in the end, the power of the alpha hellhound couldn't be denied.

Nick lowered his head and leaned heavily against Jedrek's side. Solomon waited for a long tense moment, breathing heavily and letting his power continue to flow through the room. When he finally changed back into his human form, he sent a stern glare Jedrek's way.

"Sol, meet Nick. Nick, this is my alpha, Solomon."

"This is the Chosen One's brother?"

"Yes. We have a lot to talk about."

"Yes," Solomon agreed, and the look he shot Jedrek's way sent another shiver down his spine. "But right now, we need to get Nick to the Jerricks'. Henry asked me to find Sawyer's brother and tell him about the incident."

"I was going to get to that. I was just getting more information before I told him his brothers were hurt."

And those, apparently, were the magic words. Nick made another disgruntled sound, but a moment later, he was back in his human form, trembling and shaking on the ground, but a more determined look in his eyes than Jedrek had even seen when he was fighting him back at the magic house.

"Hurt? What do you mean hurt? Who was hurt? How? How were they hurt? Where are they?" a very human Nick demanded. "Why didn't you say something earlier?" Nick scrambled to his feet and grabbed his phone. "Fuck! Six missed calls in the last hour. Why the hell did you ask me to shift?"

Jedrek ignored Solomon's questioning gaze. "For now, let's get you to your brothers."

"Right." Nick nodded and started for the door.

"Uh, Nick?" Jedrek tried to hide his smile as Nick spun around and glared. "You may want pants for this."

Nick huffed and hurried back across the room for the clothes he'd stripped off earlier. Solomon crossed his arms over his chest and glared.

"What is it with everyone and pants tonight?"

NICK

Nick rushed to get dressed while keeping an eye on the extremely powerful alpha hellhound. Jedrek was bad enough, but having the alpha standing six feet away from him had Nick's nerves screaming. He grabbed his jeans from the floor and tried to hop into them, while shooting a frustrated glare Jedrek's way.

"You should have told me right away," Nick growled. Of course, his ire did little to inspire fear when he tried to stuff both legs into one pants leg and toppled to the side. Jedrek's quick reflexes prevented him from face-planting in front of the newcomer.

"I couldn't. You weren't in control," Jedrek said softly. "I couldn't take you where they are, even after I realized who you were, until I knew you wouldn't put them in danger."

"I would never—"

"I know you wouldn't hurt your brothers intentionally, but they are surrounded by other shifters and guardians and... you need to be in control."

Nick growled again and tried to untangle his legs from his pants. He finally managed to get them on and tugged them up over his hips.

"I don't know what you're talking about. My brothers don't know about any of..." Nick paused, waving his hand around the room. "This stuff."

He didn't miss the look Jedrek and his alpha shared.

"What? What aren't you telling me?"

He grabbed his T-shirt, but his heightened senses informed him quickly that it was past time it went into the dirty clothes basket. He turned and threw it that direction before grabbing a T-shirt he'd gotten at some concert he went to with Sawyer at the college a few years before. He'd never been a fashion icon and he could give a shit less about clothes at the moment.

"Tell me," Nick demanded and he tugged the shirt over his head and into place.

"They know," Solomon said.

"No." Nick would know if they knew. They would have talked to him about it. He glanced at his phone again, thinking of the number of phone calls he'd been avoiding from them lately. "Shit. How?"

"It's a long story, Nick."

The other hellhound spoke again, and Nick's hackles rose once more. "Who the fuck are you again? And how did you get into my house?"

Jedrek squeezed Nick's arm, and it took everything he had not to tackle the hellhound again and put him in his place.

"This is my alpha, Solomon," Jedrek said. "You need to stay in control, or I will not take you to your brothers. I will not put anyone who is there with them in danger."

"I wouldn't—"

"You have no control," Solomon said. "You would."

"Sol, he's the one who set off the wards at the house. He was *there*."

Nick didn't miss the emphasis Jedrek put on the word, and they clearly had the desired effect. Solomon's brows rose, and he turned back to Nick once more.

"Someone please tell me what's wrong with my brothers."

"They were attacked during the night. Someone got through their wards. Mikey was with Sawyer at the time, and we've taken them to a special clinic where those of our kind can receive medical attention."

"Our kind?" Nick yelled. "They aren't like me...us. They need to be at a hospital."

Solomon glanced at Jedrek again.

"Stop talking to each other or whatever you're doing. It's annoying. Take me to them. I need to get them to help."

"You'll understand when we get there. Jedrek, he's your responsibility."

"Understood," Jedrek said. He glanced at Nick. "Let Sawyer explain. And stay with me. Don't get overwhelmed by your senses of all the others. Breathe."

"What are you—?"

A flaming circle opened in the middle of his living room. Solomon spared them one more warning glance before he stepped through it.

"Listen to me, Nick. *Do not lose control.* You are not going to like what you sense or smell, and I know you don't know me, but I'm telling you, your brothers are safe where they are."

"Take me to them."

Jedrek guided Nick toward the flames, and when they stepped through, Nick could barely believe his eyes. They'd gone through some sort of portal and were standing outside a really large house surrounded by a fence. On the other side, there were a ton of people milling about. There was a buzz in the air, some sort of anticipation. The lion inside of him roared in protest.

"Control, Nick. *Do not lose control.* Fight it."

"Who are they?"

"Think of them as refugees. They're looking for a safe place, too. I know you don't understand what's going on, and that your senses are being overwhelmed, but I know you can do this. We are here to help you, and as to your brother... well, he's very special. He's probably the most important person in our world, and he's very vulnerable because of it. He has special guardians to help keep him safe, but he's in constant danger. He needs you to be strong for him right now."

Nick took a moment to think and to fight for control. He pulled in breath after breath until finally he was able to form a solid thought. Jedrek hadn't been exaggerating when he said it was going to be difficult, but the news that his brothers were familiar with his world somehow lifted a weight off his shoulders. "It's Sawyer, isn't it?"

They weren't saying brothers. Both were hurt, but only one was important. Only one was vulnerable. And it wasn't difficult for Nick to figure out which brother they meant.

"Sawyer is the Chosen One."

The words rang a bell in Nick's mind, some story or other he'd heard and not paid any attention to. "I don't know what that means, but Sawyer... well, he's always been special. How does Mikey fit into this?"

"Mikey has abilities as well."

Everything he'd thought for the past several years changed in a moment. Mama Thea had always told him they were all special, but he'd never taken it to mean anything other than the obvious. She'd been their mother, their guardian and caregiver. Of course, she thought they were all special. But now, he realized she'd been trying to tell him all along.

"So what happened?"

Jedrek led him forward but stopped just outside the gate. "I don't know all the details. Let's get you inside, and you can ask for yourself."

Nick glanced at the sign by the gate and snarled. "A vet? You took my brothers to a fucking vet?"

"Nick!" Jedrek's voice had a power of its own, and Nick shook under the weight of it. "Control yourself or you can't go see them. Do you understand?"

He nodded, but the anger was still there, simmering under the surface. He didn't care who he had to get through, if his brothers needed help, he would get them to it. If they'd been hurt, they needed to be at a hospital, not with some doctor who normally treated fucking dogs and cats.

Nick looked up and saw Solomon walking their way with another man. Nick's hackles rose again. He was something else.

"That's Doctor Jerrick. *Alpha* Jerrick is the most knowledgeable doctor for our kind there is," Jedrek explained.

"I trust him with my own well-being, and that of everyone in my pack," Solomon added.

Nick sized up the doctor for a moment, remembered to breathe like Jedrek had told him, and then stepped forward. "I'm Nick Smith."

The doctor glanced down for a moment, and Nick realized he'd passed some kind of test. It hit him a second later. He'd crossed another ward.

"I'm Vaughn Jerrick." He held a hand out for Nick to shake. "Let's get you to your brothers."

Jedrek followed him like a shadow as Vaughn led Nick toward a large building to the side of the house. His instincts went bananas, as Jedrek had predicted, but Nick forced himself to remain calm. His brothers were in there, and they needed him. Several men stood guard outside the building, and none of them looked happy to see them. Vaughn opened the door and led Nick inside, but only after Sol flashed his eyes at them. They were definitely communicating somehow, and Nick had passed one more test.

"Your brothers are through here," Vaughn explained. He pushed open a door at the end of the hall and Nick was met with the sound of two swords being drawn. One of the men had curly blond hair, and the other bright blue. But they had one thing the same: they were deadly serious about keeping him away from Sawyer.

His brother was sitting up in bed, leaning against a familiar face.

"Draco," Nick rumbled.

He was shocked as hell when Draco's eyes flashed a golden color.

"Nick," Draco said.

Sword guys lowered their weapons. Nick hurried over, and Sawyer lifted his head wearily.

"What the fuck, Sawyer?" Nick grumbled.

Sawyer grabbed him and held on, his breath coming in a distressed pant. Nick let him go, then grabbed both his baby brother's cheeks in his hand. "Were you just *nuzzling* Draco? What did I tell you about that? You might catch grumpyitis or cranky fever."

Sawyer's breath steadied and he met Nick's gaze. His panic faded and he managed a grin after a moment. "You said he was the only one who'd keep me from doing stupid stuff," Sawyer sniffed. "I figured it was worth the risk."

"Damn. I did say that. Well, clearly, I was wrong." Nick waved his hand around. Sawyer smiled at him, which was what Nick was hoping for. He'd been on the edge of a freak out, and Nick had too many questions for him to wait that out. He glanced to the other side of the room at Mikey, who was surrounded by two strange men Nick didn't know at all. One was curled around Mikey's form, glaring at Nick, while the other sat on a chair beside the bed, holding his brother's hand.

"What the hell is going on, Sawyer?"

"Those are Mikey's mates, Asher and Quillon. You'd know these things if you ever returned a phone call."

Nick glared. "Don't blame this on me. I've had things and stuff."

Sawyer smirked. "You and your secrets."

"Yeah, well, what's this Chosen One crap? The only thing you're normally *chosen* for is the guy who eats the most junk food in a single sitting."

Sawyer punched his arm, but then grabbed his hand and squeezed tightly. It didn't escape Nick's notice that his hands were cold and clammy, or that they shook a bit before he tightened his hold.

"And I will always be chosen for that most sacred duty. No one can down pizza rolls like me, Nick, and don't you forget it."

Nick squeezed his hand again, looking around the room once

more. No one looked happy he was there, and he couldn't blame them. There was an underlying fear in the air, with a healthy dose of anger and confusion. "I could never forget it, baby bro."

"It's just, now I'm chosen for a few other things, too. Like saving the supernatural world. You know, just your average Tuesday."

Sawyer's voice cracked, and Draco made a rumbling sound before tugging Sawyer closer. Nick tried to make sense of what he was seeing. He took a moment to look Sawyer over more carefully, checking for any sign of injury, but other than looking exhausted, Sawyer looked okay. Mikey, on the other hand, was obviously very hurt. He had an oxygen mask over his face, and he hadn't moved once.

"What happened?"

He glanced back at Sawyer and his control slipped for just a second. He felt, more than heard, movement behind him. Sawyer gasped before breaking out into a blinding grin.

"You're a shifter? Holy shit, dude! Since when?"

The tension in the room eased and the movement behind him stopped before Nick felt the need to defend himself. He saw movement this time, out of the corner of his eye, and Jedrek appeared on the opposite side of the bed, just within his line of sight. Nick met his gaze and remembered to take a breath. *Calm. Control.* He nodded to Jedrek before turning his attention back to Sawyer.

"Since always," Nick said. "Now tell me what happened."

"No, wait," Sawyer said. "What kind of shifter are you? Tell me! I gotta know!"

Nick sighed. "Lion."

"No way!"

Nick glanced at Draco, who was staring adoringly at his brother. "He's going to ask me to roar, isn't he?"

"Or sing *The Lion Sleeps Tonight.* Could go either way."

Sawyer elbowed Draco in the side. "I'd be mad, but I did convince you to make s'mores for me."

Nick had no clue. "What?"

"Dragon," Draco said. "I lit the marshmallows on fire. It was a thing."

"You didn't," Nick said.

But of course he did. None of them could ever deny Sawyer anything. Apparently not even a... Nick gulped, stunned even in his thoughts... dragon. His brother's best friend and apparently... boyfriend?... was a dragon. Of course he was.

"Of course he did," Sawyer said. "And as to what happened... can I have a little more time before I break it all down? I mean, just know that someone tried to kill me but Mikey and my guardians saved me. And then some other stuff happened and I'm still trying to figure out what everything means so I just don't want to blab on about stuff that—"

"Sawyer, breathe," Nick demanded.

Sawyer paused and sucked in a breath. His hand tightened on Nick's and he could sense the underlying fear again.

"What's wrong with Mikey?" Nick kept his voice low and calm, but he needed answers. He needed to know who to fight for daring to lay a finger on his brothers.

"It's a magic thing. Remember how he used to see things but Mama Thea gave him that necklace and said it would help? But we always thought it was more of a... holy shit, you had a charm thing, too! I was always so jealous that she never gave me one. But she said I didn't need it, and *oh my goddess*."

"So my charm kept me from shifting, and Mikey's charm kept him from seeing bad guys."

"No, it kept him from seeing a shifter's true form," the larger man on the bed with his other brother said.

"But the guy who attacked us, well, he was really strong and Mikey's pendant thing kind of exploded and well...we think he just got overwhelmed with what he saw. Which, you know, makes sense now that I... ugh." Sawyer leaned back into Draco and tugged one of his arms around him.

Nick had always wondered why Draco put up with Sawyer. He'd

been suspicious for a long time, but Draco had never treated Sawyer with anything but respect, no matter how glaringly obvious Sawyer was about his crush. Nick had worried for a while. Now, though, Draco was looking at his brother with the complete adoration of the totally smitten. It was sweet, if a bit disturbing.

"So Mikey has two... mates? Two of 'em?"

"Yes. I'm Quillon and this is Asher," the guy sitting beside his brother said. "And we are both mated to Mikey."

"Quillon's a manticore and Asher's a dragon like Draco. Cool, huh?" Sawyer added.

Nick glared at them both. They'd get the shovel talk later. He returned his attention to his little brother.

"And you and Draco are...what? Mates as well?"

Sawyer blushed and looked around the room. "Well, see...Um... I might have more than one mate, too."

"Are you kidding me?" He heard a snort from the corner and turned his glare to Jedrek, who'd made the offending noise. "What?"

"I think your brother is the master of the understatement."

"What's that supposed to mean?"

The guys with swords from earlier came to stand by his brother's bedside. "I am Loch, fae and mate to the Chosen One."

"Andvari, vampire and mate to the Chosen One."

"Saeward, hippocamp and mate of the Chosen One."

"Eduard, griffin and mate of the Chosen One."

"Uh, Henry, mage and totally mated to Sawyer. Soooo mated to him."

Nick rolled his eyes at their joke even as the younger guy moved around him and leaned against Draco's other side.

"Very funny," Nick said.

"Not joking," Sawyer said gently. "It's part of that long story, but know that I do have multiple mates and even with everything else going on, I'm really happy."

Nick turned his glare onto all the men staring at his brother. "No way."

"Way."

He had about a million questions, but Sawyer yawned and leaned against Draco once more.

"You need to rest," Draco rumbled against Sawyer's head. He turned to Nick. "Tell him to rest."

"I need to explain—" Sawyer started, but the fear in Draco's eyes won Nick over to his side.

"Rest," Nick demanded.

As much as he wanted to know more about what was going on, the dark circles under Sawyer's eyes convinced him otherwise. He glanced at Jedrek once more and reminded himself to breathe. Besides, he had another source of information, one who'd been ordered not to leave his side and who seemed to know the game and all the players.

"But—" Sawyer began.

"I need to eat. Is there any place close by where I can grab some food?"

Draco smirked as an extremely well-dressed older guy seemed to appear from the shadows of the room. Nick hadn't even realized he was there.

"I can get you anything you require, sir."

"Uh, I can go—"

"Don't argue," Sawyer said as he smothered a yawn. "That's Cecil. He's awesome."

"Thank you, young master."

"Master?" Nick asked.

"Ugh, Cecil! I told you about that."

The older guy smirked before turning his attention to Nick. "Come with me, Mr. Smith. I'll make sure you have something to eat."

"Uh, just call me Nick. Otherwise, this just crosses the line into more weird than I can manage."

Jedrek moved toward the door, and after a final, concerned glance at his brother, Nick rose as well. "I'll be back, and I expect answers, little brother."

"Thanks for coming, Nick. I needed you here," Sawyer said.

He yawned again, and Draco tugged the blanket up over him. Sawyer closed his eyes as the others moved closer. The younger one climbed up onto the bed with him, while the blue haired guy sat on the end of the bed. The big one took Nick's place and held Sawyer's hand while the redhead and the blond moved to stand guard at the end of the bed.

Nick gave them one last look before leaving the room. Jedrek waited for him outside the door.

"I'm taking you to one of the cabins. Cecil is bringing you something to eat."

"I just said that to—"

"I need to eat, too."

Nick decided to just shut up and follow Jedrek. It wasn't like the view was bad. They went back outside where they were met with stares of awe. Most of the people began whispering to themselves while looking at him. His lion began to stir again, but Nick turned his attention to Jedrek and tuned everything else out. He memorized the width of Jedrek's shoulders and imagined them spread out beneath him. He watched the way Jedrek's ass moved beneath the snug, worn jeans that covered it. His lion had continued to stir, but it wasn't over concern at the others. No, the lion was as interested in Jedrek as Nick was. They went into a small cottage-style building a minute later and Jedrek shut the door behind them, forcing Nick to end his ogling and focus on all the questions he needed answered.

"How's your control?"

Nick wanted to lie and say he was fine, but he found himself answering honestly instead. "Shaky."

"No doubt. You did well."

Nick sucked in a breath and let it out. "I almost lost them both tonight, didn't I? And all because I refused to return their phone calls. I was too caught up in my own bullshit to be there for my brothers when they needed me."

"You're here now."

Somehow, that didn't make Nick feel better. His skin itched and he longed to let the lion free once more. Jedrek gave him a knowing look and pointed. "Go shower. It'll help you relax. I'll wait for the food."

"I don't need—"

"I need to check in with Sol and see what else is going on. You need to get cleaned up and get yourself calmed down. I always think best in the shower, anyway."

A growl built, but Nick tamped it down. "Fine."

A shower did sound good and maybe it would help him relax and get his thoughts in order. That was the only reason he was doing it. He wasn't going to let Jedrek boss him around. *No.* He was a grown man and he could take care of himself. He didn't need Jedrek to do anything for him at all. He barely even knew the man. Hellhound. Whatever. Besides, his focus needed to be on his brothers right now, and on finding out what else the hellhounds knew about the house of horrors and the kids. He wanted more than anything to know what had become of them.

He'd shower and eat and then grill the guys who seemed to have the answers.

JEDREK

J edrek waited until the water turned on and he heard Nick step into the shower before slipping out of the cabin. Both Meshaq and Solomon were waiting outside.

Neither of them said anything. Instead, they walked toward the end of the row of cottages where Vaughn and Sam had built a small playground for any visiting kids. It looked like there was a glittery powder on the see-saw, no doubt from some experiment of Ollie's gone awry.

A group of locusts chirped in the distance and Jedrek closed his eyes, listening to the sounds of the forest around him. The din of those gathered inside the wards and settled once more. So much had happened over the course of the night, and his newest discoveries only added to the mysteries they had yet to solve.

"What do you have to report?" Sol asked. "Start with why I found you fully shifted with Sawyer's brother. How did you get from the farmhouse to there?"

"Cosmo is very disgruntled, by the way," Meshaq added. "I got an earful about disrespectful lions and stubborn champions who refused backup."

Jedrek grinned. "Yeah, well, just wait until he finds out the lion was the Chosen One's brother."

Both Meshaq and Solomon grinned back at him.

"Tell us," Solomon said.

"Nick was at the house when I got there. He'd triggered the wards. Cosmo lost his mind and started attacking, which is why I sent him back here. Nick was one of them. One of the kids like Henry and Ben. He escaped. I haven't had time to find out the hows and whys, but I know he ended up with Sawyer's foster mother, and that he had another of her mysterious charms. This one kept him from shifting and suppressed his memories. He hadn't shifted in fourteen years."

Meshaq winced, and Solomon let out a low growl. "How is he not out of his mind?"

"I don't know. But his control is very shaky, so I was trying to help him when you came in. I managed to get him into a full shift to see if that would help, and that's when Solomon arrived. And if that's not enough, there was a secondary ward at the house, one that wasn't set by us. I think it messed up his shifting ability further."

Meshaq scowled. "That damn house. So let me get this straight, he shows up tonight of all nights, and he just so happens to be Sawyer's brother. The timing is very suspicious."

Jedrek couldn't deny it. He'd thought the same thing. "He said he's been searching for the house for the last few years. Apparently, his memories were on lock down after he was found until a few years ago. Like I said, I wasn't able to fully question him before Sol came and said we were needed back here."

Both alphas grew quiet, each lost in their own thoughts. Jedrek had a few questions of his own, like why he had two alphas now, but it could wait. They definitely had more pressing matters.

A twig snapped behind them, and Jedrek spun around, half shifted and ready to attack.

"Uncle Jed?" Ben asked.

"Hey, kid. What are you doing out here? Shouldn't you be inside with the others?" Jedrek forced his hellhound back, troubled that his nerves were so scattered he hadn't even paused before moving to attack.

"Yeah, well, they're all scared. So much going on, you know? First the fight at the bar, then Cosmo told Ollie that something was happening at the old house, and now with Sawyer and Mikey.... Well, no one can relax right now. Can I at least tell them everything is okay?"

"Uh, yeah. I think so?" Jedrek looked to Sol for confirmation.

Vaughn and Sam walked up and joined them. Sam wrapped an arm around his oldest son.

"Hey, Ben. What are you doing out here?" he asked.

"Just checking on everything, Papa."

Sol smiled at them and squeezed Ben's shoulder with one big hand. "You can rest easy. There was no threat to you. Or any of the children at the house."

"Did you... catch whoever it was?" Ben asked.

"Yeah. He's..." Jedrek started.

"Why don't you sit down?" Sol asked, leading Ben to sit down at the picnic table.

"Uncle Sol?"

"Sol? What's up?" Sam asked, putting himself halfway in front of his son.

"There's no easy way to say this. The person at the house was a shifter. We think..." Sol started before turning to Jedrek.

"He was there, Ben. He lived in that house for some time."

"What? That's not possible. We're all here. And no one ever— " Ben shook his head. His eyes filled with tears. "*No.*"

Jedrek knelt on the ground in front of him. He gently put his hands on Ben's knees. "He told me he's been looking for the house for a long time. Searching for you guys."

The tears Ben had been fighting off spilled over. "No. They're all dead. No one lived."

"He did, though, Ben. He finally found the house today. And now he's here. He's Sawyer's brother."

"That's impossible," Sam protested.

"Wh-what is he?" Ben asked.

"A lion."

Ben's control snapped and he began to shift. "Papa."

Sam and Vaughn both stepped in close, but it was too late. Ben began pulling at his pants while Vaughn tugged his shirt free.

"You're safe, son. We're here. Shift. Go on. You're fine. We're here. You're safe."

Within seconds, Ben was in his bear form. He stood between his fathers, snarling and shaking.

"Explain," Sam demanded.

Jedrek had no clue how to explain, but luckily he didn't have to. Solomon stepped forward. "We're gathering information still, but Nick is Sawyer's foster brother. He was found after escaping from the farmhouse almost fourteen years ago. He was given a charm blessed by the mother goddess which suppressed his memories and prevented him from shifting."

Vaughn gasped. "For how long."

"Until tonight," Jedrek said.

"That's not possible," Vaughn said. "He'd be out of his mind."

Sam didn't seem to understand but Ben let out a roar of displeasure and pulled both of their attention. Unfortunately, theirs wasn't the only attention he garnered.

"Ben!"

His brothers and sisters ran from the house with Ollie in the lead. Their eyes all glowed and they searched the area for danger. Meshaq stepped in front of Ollie and pulled him close. He was nearly frantic, and Jedrek didn't blame him. Ben had sounded awful, terrified and under threat. They all looked out for each other so much, and Jedrek had never heard Ben make a noise like he'd made moments before. He was the calm, quiet kid and had grown into a quiet, reflective young man.

"What's wrong?" Ollie demanded. "Who hurt Ben?"

"No one," Shaq said gently. "He just got a little scared. He's fine. Look at him. All of you. He's upset and needs you all to be calm and help him. Can you do that?"

Ollie nodded and Shaq opened his arms. He ran to his brother's side and dropped to his knees. "Dude, you never make noises like that. You scared me," Ollie complained. He buried his face in Ben's neck and breathed.

Jack and Emily joined him and Ben began to calm down. The only one who hadn't was Natasha. Her eyes still glowed a golden amber and her gaze darted between Meshaq and the cabin where they'd left Nick.

"Someone is here."

"Yes," Shaq explained. "A lion Ben knew from before."

"Lion?" Natasha asked. She glanced at Ben, who looked up at her with his big, sad eyes. "I'll kill him."

She started to strip off her shirt, but Shaq stilled her hand. Sam and Vaughn hurried over, and Vaughn captured her face in his hands. "I need you to wait. You obviously know who Nick is, but you don't know the whole story."

"Nick? That's his name?"

"I'll go get him," Jedrek said.

"I think that's best."

"Who the hell is Nick?" Ollie demanded. "And why are Ben and Tasha so upset? And where's Henry? I want Henry!"

"I'll get him," Solomon said.

A shrill whistle interrupted them all. Jedrek turned to find Sam with his fingers between his lips and a furious expression on his face.

"Stop. All of you stop right now. Tasha, sit down and help Ben settle. You know he needs you and that takes priority." Sam pulled out his phone and dialed. "Henry, no one is hurt, but I need you to come outside. We're over by the playground. Yes, you can bring Saeward. Tell the others they can stay with Sawyer. Meshaq, Solomon, and Jedrek are with us so you will be safe." He ended the call and turned back to them. "One of you tell me why my kids are so upset over this Nick guy."

Vaughn appeared to have already figured it out. He grabbed Sam's hand and reached for the scruff of Ben's neck with the other. Ben leaned his head into his alpha's stomach grumbling and complaining as he tried to do as Sam had asked and calm down. Jedrek looked at his alphas, who were just as shaken by all of the new developments as he was.

"Nick was one of us, Papa," Tasha said. "At least, I think he's the one that got away. I thought he was dead because he never came back. He *swore* he'd come back for us."

She finally broke and leaned more heavily into Ben's side. He howled again.

"He was at the house? He was Lion?" Ollie asked.

"Lion?" Sam asked gently. "Ben said that Lion tried to save you all. He told us stories about him."

"That was before we came, Papa," Jack said. "Only Henry, Tasha, and Ben were there with Lion, but we know he got out and never came back."

Henry reached their side just in time to hear Jack's words. "What? Lion?"

"Sawyer's brother Nick," Meshaq said. "He was at the house."

Henry paled and leaned back into Saeward. The big guardian seemed as confused as the rest of them, but he held onto Henry without speaking. "I thought he looked familiar, but I just thought it was because I'd seen pictures of him at Sawyer's house."

"It was fourteen years ago, Henry," Meshaq explained. "It's no surprise you didn't recognize him. You were young when he escaped."

"Okay," Sam said. "Has anyone bothered to explain to Nick that the kids are here?"

Jedrek shook his head.

"Then why don't you go do that before he comes out here and

gets shocked like my kids did. No more freak-outs tonight. We've had enough."

Meshaq gave him a nod, so Jedrek went back toward the cabin. He found Nick pacing around the small living area.

"What happened?" Nick demanded, the moment the door closed behind him.

"So you know how I told you we rescued the kids who were at the house?"

Nick growled, his eyes glowing.

"Nick, *control*. The kids are here. This is where we brought them. You've already met one of them. Henry. Remember him? He's one of Sawyer's mates. The younger one."

"No. That's not little Henry."

"Yes. He's grown up now. It's been fourteen years, Nick. They're all grown up now. And Tasha just told me that only three of them were there when you were."

"No," Nick said. "There were more than that. Ben and Tasha, Henry and Max. Jenny—"

Nick's voice broke and he turned away.

"Jenny?" Jedrek asked softly.

"She didn't make it. That's... that's why I knew I had to try. Tasha's here, too?"

"And Ben and Henry. Jack, Emily, and Ollie. Those are the younger ones."

Nick shook his head. "Henry. Henry was the youngest."

"No," Jedrek said. "Nick, it isn't your fault. You tried, but you were just a kid, too. They want to see you. Their dads want to meet you. But you need to make sure you're in control, okay?"

Nick looked up and pulled in a breath. Jedrek matched it, counting in his head. Deep inhale, then exhale. He waited until Nick was able to do the deeper breaths on his own and then stopped.

"Wait, you said dads?"

"You met one of them. Dr. Vaughn. Ollie managed to escape and found Sam, who brought him to Vaughn. It's a long story, but they ended up adopting all the kids. They've lived here ever since under the protection of both their pack and mine. We've kept them safe, Nick."

Nick nodded. "That's good. That's really good. This place is real nice."

"It is. Sam's a teacher. He quit working and homeschooled the kids. Ben's in med school now. He's super smart. And Tasha is just like her Nana. She's bossy and likes things her way, and she's super protective of her siblings. Henry, well, Henry is so powerful. We brought in an awen to help him with his abilities, and yeah, it kinda blew us all away how strong his powers are."

Nick began to pant and he looked at Jedrek. "Sorry," he growled before the shift began to overtake him.

"Dammit."

He waited until Nick had completed the shift before he approached. He flared his eyes and Nick let out a growl of displeasure. "You need to stay in control. I get it. You needed to shift. You aren't the only one. Ben's out there in his bear form. But you aren't getting anywhere near them until I know you're in control."

Nick snarled and took a step forward.

"Nick, I'm not fucking around. Both of my alphas are out there. So is Alpha Vaughn."

The words crept in. Jedrek could see Nick trying to process them.

"That's right. Their dad is an alpha. You really want to go tearing out there and make him think his kids are in danger? You think Henry's going to let you? That kid is strong, Nick. You should see what he can do with his magic. But trust me, you don't want him to use it against you. So calm down and we'll walk out there together. No sudden moves or I'm telling you, someone is going to take offense and you won't like what happens. Think about what you'd do if someone came up on your brothers, shifted and snarling and moving fast."

Nick growled and shook out his mane.

"I know. You'd show 'em who's boss. And that's what'll happen to you if you don't behave. Tell me you can."

Nick raised his head and there was a glimmer of humanity behind his lion eyes.

"Good. Now, let's go. Stay right beside me, and when I stop, you stop. You need to let them approach you. Ben will recognize your scent. Tasha will as well. Once they're okay with you, the others will be. You'll just have to give them a second to process. Got me?"

Nick pushed his head into Jedrek's side.

He walked to the door, and Nick did as he asked and stayed beside him. When they walked outside, the kids all made sounds, some curious, some scared. But none angry or threatened. Jedrek stopped about a dozen feet from the group and Nick stayed beside him. Ben made the first move, grumbling a complaint as he lumbered close. Nick stilled, only shaking out his mane as Ben approached. They each sniffed the air, subtly at first, and then more deeply as their animal forms recognized each other. Ben bumped his head against Nick's, and when Nick returned the gesture cautiously, it opened the door to the others.

Ollie moved to Ben's side and held onto the fur of his brother's neck. "Hey, Lion. I mean, Nick. I heard a lot about you when I was a kid."

Nick raised his head and met Ollie's gaze. They seemed to have some unspoken communication before Ollie sighed.

"It sucks that you weren't able to find us, but it turned out okay, you know? I mean, it sucked. Big time. But maybe we wouldn't have found our dads, so I think it turned out how it was supposed to. Right, Tasha?"

She approached slowly and touched Ben as well. "I hadn't thought of it like that."

"The goddess works in mysterious ways," Henry said. He stepped beside Natasha and put his arm around her. "I think she's proven that more than ever tonight."

"Yeah, well, maybe if someone would clue the rest of us into what's going on," Natasha griped.

Jedrek didn't exactly blame her. He had a couple questions he wanted answered, too.

"*Anyway*," Ollie continued, "I'm really glad you're okay, Nick. Ben always talked about how great you were. And I mean, come on, you're a fricking lion. Look at you! I've never seen a guy lion up close before. Your mane is so cool. Is that why your hair is kinda like that too? I might have been looking out the window when you came. But, um, not that your hair isn't cool. It totally is. You're *so cool*."

Jedrek couldn't believe what was happening. Nick was actually starting to preen. He fluffed out his mane and Ollie made a little sound and reached out his hand.

"Can I pet you? Is that weird? I've just... can I?"

Nick moved his head, even though it was subtle, and Ollie took it as permission. Jedrek glanced up and found everyone else watching the moment with confusion as well. Well, everyone except Vaughn. Ollie's dad didn't look confused at all. He looked amused.

"I didn't know how big lions were," Ollie said. "I mean, I kind of knew because we had a tiger here before and boy was he mean—"

Nick made a little huff of displeasure.

"I know. I mean, tigers, am I right? They're not like lions. Lions are the best. Like, you're just so regal. He was all snarly and *I'm a loner leave me alone*, but you're a pack animal like us, right? Well, a pride animal? Is that how you say it, Dad?"

"That works, Ollie," Vaughn said.

"Jack, look," Ollie said. "His mane is so awesome."

Jack moved closer, too, and Emily followed. Even though they weren't exactly kids anymore— Ollie had just turned nineteen and Emily and Jack were in their shared months of being twenty— they had a childlike way about them that was hard to ignore. Of course, they were teenagers, too. Like Jack comparing Nick's mane to Natasha's hair when she woke up in the morning and earning himself a smack on the head.

Nick reacted by bumping his head against Jack and huffing.

Jack looked sheepish. "Sorry, Tasha."

"What is happening right now?" Sam whispered in awe.

"It's okay. My hair *is* kinda crazy in the mornings."

Ben leaned into her and she looped her arm around his neck.

"Ben said you used to roar at them when they came to get us," Tasha said quietly. "I kinda remember but I kinda don't, you know? Like I've blocked a lot of that stuff away and I don't want to really remember. But he used to tell us how amazing it was. And how scared they were of you. And how when they made you stay like a lion, they regretted it because you were so terrifying. I wish I remembered that part."

"And then Ben would do it to them, too," Emily said quietly. "They hated it when he shifted and never liked for him to do it. But when they got really mean, he would and he said he was doing what you did to keep them in line. So thanks for protecting us, too."

Jedrek tightened the hold he had on Nick's mane, unable to resist sending him some kind of message as well. Everyone standing around them was affected by their words. The kids rarely talked about their time as hostages, about what had happened to them in those days.

Henry leaned down and wrapped his arms around Nick's neck. "Thank you, Nick. I have to go back inside now, but will you come visit me soon? If you want to? I mean, I'd like that if you could."

Nick made a little sound of agreement and all the kids leaned in, joining in the group hug.

"Things are really crazy right now, but it makes me feel better to know you're here," Henry continued. "I feel safer. Isn't that crazy? My mates are super strong and I know they'll keep me safe, but it's because you're here, Lion. I mean, Nick. Sorry. You're still Lion in my head."

Nick leaned into him and nuzzled his head against Henry, who sighed before pulling away.

"I need to get back to my mate now. Oh, he's your brother. Duh. Sorry. How crazy is that? So you'll definitely come visit, huh? How crazy is it that my Lion is Sawyer's brother? Oh and I was supposed to tell you that Cecil will be bringing food soon because Nana was in the middle of something in the kitchen and you know how she gets. Well, actually, you don't know. Goddess, I'm tired. But trust me, Nana doesn't let anyone in her kitchen when she's in the middle of something so he'll be here soon."

"Speaking of tired, you all need to get to bed. Even you, Ben. Don't give me that look. It's been a long day and we need you tomorrow to help in the clinic. If you aren't quite ready to shift back, you can sleep in our room tonight in your bear form."

Ben grumbled.

"I am not treating you like a kid, young man. I am treating you like someone who had one hell of a day. In fact, I think we're having a living room sleepover fest tonight. Who's with me?"

"Me," Ollie said.

Sam smiled and held out his hand. "Come on."

Ollie snuck one last hug before moving to his Papa's side. All the kids made sure to snuggle up to Nick a little more before they left, even Ben. There would be a lot more conversations coming Nick's way, Jedrek had no doubt, but it was definitely moving in the right direction.

At least, it was until Henry stiffened and his guardian reacted, turning into the biggest damn horse Jedrek had ever seen in his life. Nick reacted as well, putting himself in front of Jedrek and roaring in the direction Henry had turned.

"Meshaq!"

Henry sighed. "It's okay guys. It's Zaire. But boy is she pissed. We should probably go inside. Um, quickly."

"Us, too," Sam said.

The kids followed Sam and Vaughn back toward the house, but only after Ben pushed against Nick one last time. Once they'd moved away, Nick leaned heavily into Jedrek's legs and he stroked his neck softly. "You did great," he whispered quietly. "Now watch because

Zaire is the only person on the planet who can take Meshaq down a notch. Well, except the goddess, but you know... it's wild."

"I am going to skin you, you mangy mutt!"

Zaire stormed their way, her eyes blazing and her magic swirling around her. Jedrek continued touching Nick, keeping him calm even as her power drifted their way. Her ire wasn't directed at them anyway.

NICK

Nick never really considered himself a feelings kind of guy. He was the one who provided logic and general insight. If you wanted someone to cry and wail and call your stupid ex names, go somewhere else. If you wanted help getting to a solution and talking through options, Nick was your man.

Except.

In his lion form, Nick *felt*. Every touch of Jedrek's hand on his neck sent electricity down his spine. He wanted to shove closer, to inhale his crisp, deep scent and wallow in it. The human side of his mind got it. He'd attached to Jedrek as the first person he'd shifted with, so it made him safe. It was logical but so intense it was disconcerting.

Memories of his youth rolled through him as well, and seeing the kids he'd left behind all grown up had nearly brought him to his knees. They looked happy, smelled healthy, and had clearly grown up surrounded by love. Their alpha was a steady presence, his power strong and true. Nick accepted it as safe within moments. The human one, *Sam*, Nick's human side provided, had been even more fierce in his protection of his cubs and Nick's lion approved of him as well. The hellhound alphas, on the other hand, had so much power they felt threatening. Every time Nick caught their scent, he wanted to roar and herd Jedrek away from them. Which made absolutely no sense.

When the witch came, Nick first heard the uptick of Henry's heart, that slight burst of panic and fear. He'd reacted the same way Henry's mate had. *Protect. Defend. Attack.* But Henry's quick words kept Nick's lion from taking control. The witch was strong and her magic smelled of fire and burning wood. But Jedrek's hand stayed calm and sure on his side. He wasn't afraid. He was amused.

Henry's mate, on the other hand, wasn't happy in her presence. He pranced between them until Henry finally grabbed his mane and touched their heads together. "I'm fine," Henry whispered. "She's not mad at me. She's gonna tear a strip off Uncle Meshaq's hide, though. Come on. Change back and watch the carnage with me. It'll be fun."

The witch stopped, her black hair flying about her in messy curls. She was older, but definitely not old. There was something timeless and immeasurable about her. Nick inhaled, trying to process what his senses were trying to tell him, but his human brain didn't have the answers he sought. And his lion simply understood that she was a threat.

"Zaire, cut it out. You're making my magic wonky," Henry complained. He skirted around his mate and approached her. Nick started to take a step forward to protest, but Jedrek's hand tightened on his neck. He growled a complaint and Jedrek dropped to one knee in response. He felt better with him at this level. He was easier to protect. And closer. And he smelled better this way. Nick wanted him on the ground so he could cover him and it made no sense. He'd felt that way before as well. He needed to look into lions a bit more. He'd avoided it before, and it was one more thing to add to his list of regrets.

"That's Zaire, Henry's mentor," Jedrek said quietly. "And she's pissed because Solomon brought her son into a fight we had last night. And damn, it's been a long-assed day."

"Henry," Zaire said. "You look... great goddess, is that a hippocamp?"

"Yeah," Henry said as he pulled her into a hug. "He's one of my mates."

"You never do things by halves, do you boy?"

"Nope. You taught me better than that."

She grinned then, and the scent of her magic changed. Settled. Simmered instead of burned.

"See?" Jedrek whispered. "She's okay. Just ticked off at my alphas."

"I did teach you better than that," Zaire continued. "Someone needs to tell me what the flying hell is going on around here."

Henry sighed. "They can catch you up. Sawyer's hurt so... we need to get back inside."

"Hurt? You need me?"

Henry hugged her again. "No. He'll be okay. I'll talk to you after you yell at Uncle Meshaq, though."

"Sounds good, honey. Now," Zaire said as she turned and pointed one long, black painted nail at Saeward. "You get him inside. He's exhausted and his magic is out of sorts. I demand you take care of him."

Saeward shifted back and lowered his head reverently. "Yes ma'am. He was resting but his family required his presence."

She huffed. "Henry, no excuses. You know you can't get exhausted like this. I also taught you better than that."

Henry nodded and moved to Saeward's side. "I'll go sleep."

Zaire turned again and finally caught sight of Nick.

She stared him down.

He refused to blink. A growl built deep in his chest. He stepped forward, ignoring the tug from Jedrek's hand. He would not be the first to look away. She would accept him as her equal or she would feel his teeth on her neck.

"Well, aren't you a feisty one. But your magic is really fucked up."

She stepped closer as well and Nick let out a warning growl. "Son, you better bring your human side back to the front, because I do not take kindly to shifters showing me their teeth."

She thought she was stronger than him? She thought she could take him in a fight? Nick snarled.

"Hmm. You don't know any better, do you? Interesting. I know this magic, don't I? Meshaq, speak."

"I'm not your dog to command, Zaire."

"And yet, you spoke on command."

Jedrek snickered beside him and Nick's tension eased a bit. He took a step back, crowding closer, and Jedrek grabbed his mane again. "Their fights are epic," Jedrek said. "You'd think they were siblings. Sometimes, I think they are. I see how Tasha bosses her brothers around and I see Zaire and Meshaq. You haven't met Calli, yet. She's one of my pack and is strong like this, too. They both trained Tasha. Don't let her pretty fool you, not that you would. Tasha could totally kick your ass."

Nick snarled again, unable to resist. Jedrek must think him weak. It wouldn't do. He needed to show him his strength. Prove himself.

"No, no. I don't mean it that way," Jedrek said. "Just that she's tough, you know? She came out of that house and wanted to be strong, right?"

Nick's ire faded a bit. He wanted Tasha to be strong, to be able to face any threat that headed her way. His human side crept forward again, happy that the little fox he'd left behind had become such a strong young woman. And if this witch had helped her, maybe she would be okay, too. She'd shared her strength with one of his. That made her acceptable, at least for now. He would give her a chance. He turned his attention back to the staring match going on between Zaire and Meshaq. It stretched for a long moment, until smiles broke over both of their faces.

"I'm still mad at you. Where's Drew?"

"Sleeping."

"I always knew he was the smart one of the group." Zaire turned her attention to Solomon and scowled. "What the hell? Another alpha? One wasn't enough for you guys?"

Solomon grinned and stepped forward. "The goddess had a different plan."

Zaire huffed. "Why does that one smell like black magic?"

She'd pointed at Nick, but her focus remained on the hellhounds. Nick didn't like it. He was the threat. She should be paying attention to him.

"Steady," Jedrek whispered. "Let her talk to them. You can't exactly answer her questions right now, and trust me, this news is best from them. She's gonna be pissed. She helped save the kids. Those wards are hers, both here and at the old house. Well, one of them is. I'll tell you more later. Or they will. Damn, I'm so exhausted I can't even make sense."

Jedrek yawned widely, and Nick gave him a little nudge toward the cabin.

"No, I'll wait with you. She's gonna want to talk to you, but then I'll go sleep, okay?"

Nick huffed. Stubborn man.

"Zaire," Jedrek said and the witch turned her attention back to them. "I know you're pissed, but can it wait a sec? Something weird happened tonight out at the old farmhouse. I was going to ask my alphas to contact you."

"Why were you at the old farmhouse?" Zaire asked.

Nick tried not to lose control as her magic flared brighter once more. Her anger was a physical thing that changed the very air around them.

"The ward went off. Uh, Nick set it off actually and before you freak out, he was one of them, Zaire. Did Henry ever tell you about Lion?"

Her eyes flicked to Nick. He snarled in reply. "This is the boy who they thought killed trying to escape?"

"Yes," Jedrek said. "He was found by Sawyer's foster mother. Nick is Sawyer's older brother."

"Oh really? Now isn't that an interesting turn of events."

Zaire came closer and leaned down so she was in Nick's face. He didn't like it, but something in him stilled. He sensed curiosity touching him, almost as if her magic circled him, checking for answers. Proving his story. And part of him wanted that. Someone else to back him up and say *yes, this is him. He was there.* None of it felt entirely real, especially in this form. But Nick wasn't ready to go back to two legs yet. No, he wanted the strength of his lion instead.

"My friend, you need help, don't you? Hmm. Jedrek, what was it that caused your concern?"

"There was a second ward at the farmhouse. One I hadn't seen before, but of course, the wards haven't been triggered in quite some time. I think it did something to Nick's ability to shift."

She pushed up again and returned her attention to the alphas. "This might be the break we've been waiting for. With the remnants on the lion and a ward I can break apart..."

Both Meshaq and Solomon's eyes flared red. "We can find those responsible?"

She grinned and Nick couldn't help taking a step back. He made sure Jedrek was close, shielded from the dangerous presence in front of them.

"We finally have a chance."

Nick trembled. The powerful surge of magic came from all sides. Even Jedrek seemed empowered by her words. And Nick got it. At least the human side of him did. If they'd been trying to find who'd hurt them as kids for all this time, they had to be as angry and frustrated as Nick had been for all those years. She turned to Nick and her smile was feral. "I'm going to get them, Lion. I will make them pay for what they did to you and the others."

He snarled, but it wasn't to threaten her. She understood.

"Jedrek, he needs to sleep. His magic is a mess. He seems to be attached to you."

"Yes," Jedrek answered.

"Meshaq?"

"Oh, finally acknowledging that I'm the alpha here, huh?" Meshaq asked.

She arched a brow.

"Fine. Jedrek, stay with Nick. We're going to go check out the farmhouse. Get some rest and stay within the wards. Drew is sleeping—"

"So is Cody."

"I'll keep watch over your mates," Jedrek said.

"Thank you. Cecil is bringing food, so you guys eat, and then get Walt and Calli up for the next watch."

"Understood."

Solomon leaned down closer to Nick and looked into his eyes. "I'm trusting you. This is my pack and my family. My mate is in a cabin next to yours. You will not be given a second chance. Do you understand?"

His lion moved inside him. He was being spoken to alpha to alpha. Extended a trust that he shouldn't be. Nick huffed, and Solomon gave him a nod before turning and walking back toward Meshaq and Zaire. Another of the flaming circles opened and the three of them walked through. The portal vanished moments later.

"Come on," Jedrek said. "We need to get you back to human form so you can eat."

So *they* could eat. Nick gave Jedrek a push with his head before walking toward the cabin. Jedrek opened the door and Nick walked through before turning to look at him. Once the door was closed, Jedrek knelt down in front of him once more. Their eyes met. Nick's lion preened. He wanted to compliment Jedrek's eyes, such a stormy gray. Tell him that the mohawk was both fierce and sexy. Comment on the breadth of his shoulders, proving his strength. Nick couldn't help but snarl. He wanted to bond with this man, to—

The shift overtook him, as fast as when he'd heard the news of his brothers. He *needed* to be human. To use his human words, process his thoughts with more of his human mind. He knelt before Jedrek moments later, gasping for breath but back in his human form.

"What the hell?"

"You're very fast," Jedrek said.

Nick continued to breathe, focusing on the man in front of him as if he were an oasis in the desert. And he desperately needed a drink. His instincts raged. His breath quickened. His cock twitched, awakening a deep need. He wanted. He could smell the desire in the air.

"Get dressed, Nick."

A growl built in his chest, but a knock on the door startled him enough that it pulled his focus.

"Smell the food. You need to eat. Get your clothes on unless you want Cecil seeing what the goddess gave you."

Nick huffed and grabbed the sweatpants he'd found earlier. He didn't know who they belonged to, but everything in the drawers seemed generic and up for grabs. He jammed his legs inside as Jedrek moved to the door. Cecil stood on the other side, looking highly amused for some reason. He carried a tray inside and set it on the counter of the mini kitchen.

"My apologies for the delay, gentlemen. I am not in my own home, so must abide by the needs of my host."

It took Nick a second to find words. He resisted the urge just to huff again. Jedrek seemed to understand him that way, but he didn't think Cecil would. "Thank you."

"You're very welcome. Your brothers are resting comfortably. I took the liberty of peeking in on them while the food was being prepared."

"Good. You seem to know a lot about all this," Nick said.

"I consider your brother my oldest and dearest friend."

"Huh," Nick said as Cecil put food onto a plate for him. He couldn't figure this guy out. And he didn't want to be served. "I can do that myself."

"Sit."

Nick shrugged and pulled out a chair at the two-person table against the wall. Cecil handed him the plate and placed a napkin-rolled set of utensils beside it. "Draco's his oldest friend. And I suppose dearest. Not you."

Cecil smiled, but it was one of those knowing ones that Nick always found frustrating.

"You know too much, don't you?" Nick asked.

He didn't get an answer. Cecil turned and prepared another plate before placing it on the other side of the table. "Jedrek?"

"Yeah, I can eat. Thanks, Cecil."

Nick couldn't stop looking at the butler guy. Something about him... it was weird. It was like Nick didn't want to look at him, but he couldn't exactly stop. Something urged him to look away. *Nothing to see here.* But he fought that urge. Cecil didn't exactly scream predator, but he definitely wasn't prey either. He was something else. Something different. Another thing Nick didn't have the words for even though his newly heightened instincts were trying to tell him to pay attention.

They each got a glass of some iced fruity tea thing. Nick sniffed it but couldn't quite identify what it was.

"Your brother is more than what you know," Cecil said quietly. "And he needs you at your fittest for the coming struggles he faces."

Nick glanced up from his plate. He hadn't even realized he'd looked away. He met the older man's gaze and saw wisdom. Strength. Courage. Pride. He liked what he saw. "I'll do what it takes."

"Good," Cecil said. "Listen to the hellhounds. They will help you become what you were meant to be. And now, I will leave you to your dinner. Please don't hesitate to find me if there is anything else you require."

He gave Nick another significant look before walking out the door. Nick forced himself to keep looking until Cecil's path took him out of the line of sight of the doorway. Which he'd left open. On purpose. Like he knew Nick would be watching. Nick turned his attention back to Jedrek who'd lifted the glass of fruity whatever and taken a curious sip.

"What is it?" Nick asked.

"Dunno. And for that matter, no, I don't know what Cecil is either. I've learned that when it comes to your brother, it's best to just not ask questions."

"Seriously? Sawyer's just... I mean, he's just a kid. You know?"

"He's not a kid, Nick. He's got some of the most powerful of our kind as mates, and he's got a pretty big destiny."

"Yeah. Saving the world. I thought that was the hellhounds' job."

Jedrek shrugged and lifted his sandwich. It looked like a BLT. And just the way Nick liked them, too. Heavy on the B. Easy on the L. He watched Jedrek chew for a second then lick a stray drop of mayo from his lips. Another growl built. Nick forced himself to look down at his own plate.

"Your instincts are playing havoc with you. It's okay. Don't worry about it," Jedrek said. "Just eat and then you can get some sleep. It'll settle down."

But Nick didn't think it would. He had a feeling that this thing inside him came from some place much deeper, a place the dark magic hadn't touched. A place that belonged to him and his lion and no one else. He picked up his sandwich and took a bite, savoring the perfectly crisp bacon and ice-cold tomato.

"Stuff like this happens sometimes when a shifter is injured," Jedrek said. He poked at the pasta salad on his plate before returning to the sandwich for a second bite.

Nick chewed and watched.

Jedrek swallowed again and met Nick's gaze. "Eat, Nick."

Nick nodded and returned his attention to the food. His instincts were speaking to him, and he had a curious feeling he was going to like what they told him.

JEDREK

It took Jedrek a couple seconds to remember where he was when he woke up. It took him another couple to realize he wasn't alone. He was on his belly with one leg curled up against the mattress. He had a weight across his back and a muscular thigh tucked between his legs. He moved, slowly and cautiously, only to hear an annoyed growl. The weight on him shifted and an arm crept around and then under him, pinning him in place.

He'd be pissed if he hadn't recognized that growl. *Nick.*

They'd both passed out after eating. Although... if memory served, Jedrek had forced Nick to take the bed and he'd stretched out on the couch. It had been well into the morning before Nick had wound down enough to actually sleep, but by that time Jedrek was ready to drop. He'd been up for almost two straight days and had taken on a pack of aswangs in the meantime. He'd healed a pretty serious injury and fought off a deranged lion for good measure.

He'd been tired.

But he'd not been in bed with Nick.

"Nick," Jedrek said. "Lemme up."

"Sleep," Nick grumbled. "Shhh."

Nick nuzzled the back of his neck before his hot breath began sending tendrils of desire down Jedrek's spine. He really needed to calm down. Nick was off limits. Damaged by magic and dealing with instincts he wasn't understanding. Plus, he was the Chosen One's brother, and that way lay madness.

"I need to pee," Jedrek said, even though it was only halfway true. He did need to use the bathroom, but he could have waited. He was comfortable and warm, and still a little sleepy.

Another growl. Nick's hand stroked his chest before creeping down to his stomach. Jedrek couldn't help but shiver against the touch.

"Shhh," Nick repeated before he let out a muffled snore.

Jedrek's instincts were going crazy. He didn't let anyone touch his stomach, and yet, Nick's hand splayed there like he owned it. His thumb moved slowly, caressing bare skin. His fingers curled into the trail of hair leading down. He couldn't help but tighten his stomach, and Nick's thumb stilled. Jedrek sucked in a breath and reached for Nick's wrist. He needed to move.

Nick moved faster, rolling onto him and pinning him to the mattress. Another low growl filled the room and Jedrek groaned. He wished he could say there wasn't any desire in the sound, but he'd be lying. It was a mixture of *want* and *dear goddess what am I doing?*

Needless to say, the dear goddess portion of his thoughts won. In a well-practiced move, he grabbed Nick's wrist and rolled, flipping him off the bed. Nick landed on the floor with a clatter, and Jedrek flipped off the bed and crouched over him. He put his clawed hand against Nick's neck and flared his eyes.

"Jed?" Nick rumbled sleepily. "Ow."

He raised his hand and instead of claws, human fingers rubbed the back of his head.

"You with me?"

"Clearly? Is something happening? Is Sawyer okay?"

Nick woke quickly as his thoughts began to race, and Jedrek

tightened his hold. "They're fine. I thought you were going to shift in your sleep."

Nick scowled. "So you threw me on the floor?"

When he put it that way...

"Sorry. I'm going to... uh, go clean up and... uh, check on the others."

"Good plan. I wonder if my brothers are awake yet."

Jedrek pushed to his feet and tried to ignore the way his body hummed at the sight of Nick sprawled sleepily on his back. "We can go find out."

"And hey, are your alphas and... what's her name?"

"Zaire?" Jedrek paused and took a deep breath. "Yes, my alphas are back."

"Did you just smell for them?"

Jedrek glanced at Nick and found him staring at him with a mixture of curiosity and awe. "Yeah."

Nick stared at him, then inhaled deeply. "Fuck, you smell so good," Nick groaned.

And that didn't help matters.

"Let's go check in with the others," Jedrek said. He grabbed his clothes from where he'd left them on the table after changing into another pair of the sweatpants provided by the clinic the night before.

"You think you could take me back to mine so I can get some clean clothes?" Nick asked. He'd grabbed his clothes as well as was staring at them with his nose scrunched up.

"They're fine. Your senses are heightened right now. Just put 'em on. I'll be back in a sec."

Jedrek escaped to the bathroom and closed the door behind him. He splashed cold water on his face and stared at his reflection. After giving himself a stern, but silent, lecture to get his shit together, Jedrek got himself ready for the day using one of the spare toiletry sets stored under the sink.

When he went back into the main room, he found Nick staring

out the window. "I must have been really out of it last night," Nick said. "I mean, part of me knew there were other people out there, but I didn't even process it. I was so focused on getting past the alphas and getting to my brothers, that I didn't even see them."

"They weren't threats to you," Jedrek explained. The crowd had actually thinned a little, but there were still a bunch of folks huddled around. "Come on. I'll take you to see your brothers."

Nick followed him out of the cabin, his attention focused on the clinic already. They found Draco standing outside the door.

"Sawyer?" Nick asked quickly.

"Being a pain in the ass."

"Which means he's fine. Mikey?"

"No change."

Nick made one of his many noises and glanced at Jedrek. "I'm going to go see them."

Jedrek nodded. "I need to find my alphas. Stay inside the clinic. Draco?"

Draco looked between him and Nick for a moment. "I'll stay with him."

"Thanks."

"Meshaq is up at the main house with Zaire and the others."

Jedrek nodded and shared one more look with Nick. "I'll be back in a bit."

Nick huffed and turned to go inside.

Jedrek pretended he didn't know exactly what that sound meant as well.

Sam and the kids were making rounds outside in the yard. Drew and Cody were with them, along with Teague and Achim. His other pack members looked good, much better than they had the night before. They'd come through the battle without any loses thanks to Solomon's quick thinking. The other champions were still around as well. Jedrek could feel their energy. There was a lot of power gathered within these wards, and the thought of it sent a thread of anxiety through him.

He knocked on the door of the main house and heard his alpha's voice inviting him inside. He poked his head in the door first, and found them all gathered at the long dining room table where Sam, Vaughn, and their kids normally ate. But instead of being surrounded by his family, Vaughn had Meshaq, Solomon, Zaire, Eduard, and Andvari seated with him. It was a war council if Jedrek had ever seen one.

"Come sit," Vaughn offered.

They had a table full of food in front of them, no doubt courtesy of Vaughn's grandmother. Nana always took care of all of them, and with Cecil's help on the side, no doubt they were managing to feed the entire crowd without breaking a sweat.

Jedrek sat down beside Solomon in one of the few empty seats left at the table. Solomon pushed a bowl of something amazing smelling at him and Jedrek accepted it happily.

Solomon leaned in. "We just got back. Everything go okay?"

"Yeah. We passed out. Nothing happened."

Nothing he needed to tell his alpha about, anyway. Although they might be having a discussion soon about Jedrek's apparent lack of control.

Solomon grabbed the back of his neck and squeezed. "You look better."

"I actually got some sleep. Unlike you. You look like crap," Jedrek teased.

"And don't think Cody hasn't given me an earful about it." Solomon didn't look like he minded one bit. "I want you here for this, okay?"

It wasn't unusual for their alpha to have one of them sitting in on an important gathering like this, but it wasn't normally Jedrek. Calli or Solomon were the first Meshaq called upon. He felt a surge of something he'd never felt before and couldn't quite identify. Pride. Power. Purpose.

"We might as well get started," Meshaq said. "Last night, major changes happened in our world. Doors unlocked which had been closed for a long time, and many of our lives were rewritten."

Jedrek glanced around the table. Yeah, some shit had gone down, but this sounded bigger than that.

"We don't know much," Eduard said. The griffin was one of the more level-headed of Sawyer's guardians.

"Don't stall," Zaire said sharply. "Spit it out already."

Eduard wasn't fazed by her in the slightest. He glanced at her, waiting for her to calm, before continuing. "Sawyer is actually the son of the mother goddess."

Jedrek wasn't sure he heard him clearly.

"That means..." Vaughn began, but his voice drifted off.

"He is equal to our goddess, her brother," Meshaq added.

"Wait, what?" Jedrek asked.

"Fuck my life," Zaire groaned. "And last night, who exactly attacked him?"

"Their other brother," Andvari added. The vampire sounded on the verge of snapping.

Eduard touched his arm before speaking again. "Unfortunately, Sawyer's memories have been taken and the mother has informed us that he will not be getting them back."

"I'm so confused," Jedrek said. "Does that mean Nick...?"

"No," Meshaq said. "Nick and Mikey are both foster brothers, but no more. We don't know who Mama Thea was, but she seems to have collected three powerful strays."

"Collected," Vaughn said. "I'm not sure I like that choice of word."

"But that does appear to be the right word, doesn't it?" Zaire didn't seem impressed either.

"As a result of the attack on Sawyer and the inevitability of his true status getting out, my goddess has given me... a promotion." Meshaq didn't look comfortable with the word. He looked around the table for a moment before continuing. "She has asked that Drew and

I perform some other duties for her, and has given over the control of the hellhounds to Solomon."

"But Meshaq is still an alpha," Solomon said. "He is the alpha of all of our kind now. His powers have been extended to beyond this realm and the goddesses have honored him with this power."

Zaire smirked and leaned forward. "Proud of him, are we?"

Solomon growled at her and flashed his eyes. "I am."

"So am I. No one deserves it more. But I'm a bit confused as to why you're taking your human mate along for the ride. You sure that's safe?"

Meshaq's eyes burned and Jedrek trembled at the sheer power rolling off of him. "No one will harm my mate."

"Whoa," Zaire said. "Where'd that come from?"

Meshaq grinned and Jedrek was reminded once again of their long friendship. Zaire always poked the beast, but at the end of the day, she had trusted Meshaq with her life and the life of her son. Which reminded Jedrek that he hadn't seen or heard her chew him out for involving Keziah in the fight against the aswang.

"So," Vaughn said. "We have a human who's actually a god, our champion has been called away, a new champion installed, and we found out the Chosen One's brothers both have powers of their own."

"And let's not forget that Nick arrived when he did," Zaire said.

"Or the other lions," Vaughn said.

"Other lions?" Zaire asked. "What the hell, Meshaq? Didn't you think that was significant?"

Meshaq pointed at Solomon. "It's his fault."

Eduard chuckled. "We can yell about that later. Andvari and I want to get back to our mates. What can you tell us about the wards at the old house? Sawyer will want to know that his brother is safe."

"I gathered some of the magic but will need some time to break it apart. It is strong and dark. But I will find them. Speaking of safe," Zaire turned her glare to Solomon, "now that you've involved my son and his coven in this mess, you are honor bound to provide protection to them."

"We will," Solomon said.

Zaire returned her glare to Meshaq. "This is all your fault. He's not as fun to argue with as you are."

Jedrek shook his head, but the moment lifted the heavy atmosphere just enough to allow them all to take an easy breath.

"We can't keep this many people here," Vaughn said. "We'd be a beacon for trouble and it would put my patients at risk. I want to help, but I also have a duty. Our community depends on this being a safe place."

"We will be returning home," Eduard said. "Sawyer is already itching to go, but he doesn't want to leave his brother's side."

Jedrek wasn't sure they could convince either of Mikey's brothers to leave his side.

"I can talk to him," Vaughn said.

"And I'd like the lion to come with me," Zaire said. "His magic is more changed than the others. If I can figure out why, it may give me another clue."

Solomon and Meshaq shared a glance, and Jedrek didn't even have to wonder what they were thinking before they said it.

"Jedrek and Nick will go with you," Solomon said. "I'll work on finding safe places for the others."

"I only have a few more hours before I must return to the gate. The goddess gave me until sunset," Meshaq explained.

"What's going to happen to the bar?" Vaughn asked.

"The others will run it. I'm sure we can find a few volunteers to help out." Solomon turned to him. "Jedrek?"

"I'll make it work," Jedrek said.

Solomon squeezed his neck once more. "Check on Izzy for me, will you?"

Jedrek nodded. One of their human packmates, Izzy, had been staying with the coven with her daughter since finding out their world existed. She'd been in shock, and her kid had been in danger. She'd needed a time out, but they'd needed her to be safe. Solomon had her taken to the coven until she decided what she wanted to do.

"I will," Jedrek said. "What about the lion cubs?"

Solomon rubbed his eyes tiredly. Leandra and her cubs were refugees, but they'd also been affected by the same magic that had touched Nick and the rest of the kids. There were a lot of moving pieces on the board, and it was becoming hard to keep up with it all.

"Zaire and I will talk, and we'll see what Leandra wants to do."

"I want to find them, Alpha," Jedrek said. He couldn't keep his eyes from flaring and Solomon's burned in reply.

"We will. And they will pay for what they've done. The goddess has promised us that. Go home and pack. I'm not going to rotate you all in and out of the coven's place like we do here at the clinic. It's not safe. You'll stay there and I'll come check on you myself as soon as I'm able."

Jedrek nodded and stood. "I'll be back soon."

Meshaq rose and followed him to the door. "Solomon told me how well you did in the fight. Stay strong, and listen to your instincts."

Jedrek met his gaze and breathed. "I will."

"They won't lead you astray," Meshaq said with a knowing smile before he hooked his hand around Jedrek's neck and touched their foreheads together. "And I won't even tell Drew what's happening. I'll let you do it."

Even though his voice was lowered, Jedrek couldn't help looking around to make sure no one else had overheard. "Nothing is happening," Jedrek protested.

"Uh-huh. Drew saved you some doughnuts. He put them in the oven in our cabin so no one would touch them. He felt bad that you were called away earlier."

Jedrek grinned. "How's he going to handle all this?"

"Probably better than me. He's looking forward to the adventure, but I'm dreading leaving my pack. Of course, I don't think it's sunk in with him yet that he won't be nagging you guys every day so... we'll see how it goes when he realizes."

"Better you than me. Wonder if you can text between realms. How will he survive without all the news?"

Meshaq shivered. "In all seriousness, if you need me, I will find a way. I've spoken to Solomon already, but I want the rest of you to know as well. No matter where my duties for the goddess takes me, you are still my pack."

"This isn't goodbye, Meshaq," Jedrek said. "It's see you later."

Meshaq scowled. "This is one of those pop culture references I don't get, isn't it?"

"Possibly. Now, I've gotta go. My alpha gave me an order."

He got one last neck squeeze before Meshaq released him. Jedrek hurried outside, shot a quick look toward the clinic but didn't see Nick, and then opened a portal. He had no idea what he needed to bring, but from the sounds of things, he'd be with Zaire and the coven for a while. He gathered enough clothes for a week or two, then tossed his tablet and chargers into the bag. He rummaged in the kitchen for his favorite protein bars— he didn't care what Drew said, they didn't taste like dirt— and added those as well. He also grabbed a few of his favorite movies and after another thought, he unplugged his Blu-Ray player and added it to the bag as well. Knowing Zaire, having Internet wouldn't be considered "safe" so poor Keziah had probably grown up without. He groaned and grabbed another bag, adding a few books he'd been meaning to get around to. He was probably going to be stuck in some weird commune where they didn't even have power. They probably didn't even eat meat.

Jedrek tried not to pout as he went back through his house one last time. He grabbed his supplies from the bathroom, including his clippers to keep the mohawk in shape, and then stared at the lower drawer of the bathroom cabinet. He was working. This was his job. And yeah, it wasn't a typical human type job, but he served a goddess and did a damn fine job of it. He wouldn't put that at risk. No matter what. He was there to protect and to serve.

But he'd been told to listen to his instincts.

Jedrek opened the drawer and grabbed a bottle of lube and a

sleeve of condoms. They didn't need the rubbers, but Nick might not know that and Jedrek didn't want what might be happening to get derailed because of that. He'd slept with enough humans to know they took their safety seriously and he didn't blame them. He couldn't exactly say *supernatural creature here. Disease free. Trust me.*

Not that anything would happen. But it was better to be prepared, just in case. He stopped thinking and stuffed the supplies into the bottom of his bag. He watered his plants and locked up the house before grabbing both bags and reopening the portal. He walked into chaos, and the sound of a very pissed off lion roaring.

NICK

To say that Nick was angry when he found out exactly how much danger Sawyer was in was the understatement of the century. He made it through the entire explanation— his brother, a god?— before he realized that this was more than just some random attack. Someone— another freaking god from the sounds of things— was trying to kill his brother. And that's when he lost control. He felt it coming. The signs were there. He ran out of the clinic with Draco on his heels. He made it to the door, then out onto the grass. And then he shifted. He was immediately a tangle of sweatpants and old T-shirt.

His senses were immediately overwhelmed by the scent of other shifters. Powerful creatures. Alphas. Warriors. They were all there. Threats to his brothers, lying just inside the doors, weakened and vulnerable. He roared, trying to free himself from the tangle of fabric. No one would hurt his pride. No one. His brothers would be safe. He would make sure of it.

"Nick!"

The voice was somewhat familiar but still a threat. He burned and the underlying scent reminded him that he faced a dragon. Yet he remained vulnerable in his human form. Foolish dragon. Nick's muscles clenched and he prepared to launch himself at the dangerous creature before him.

"Nick!"

Another voice, this one more intriguing. *Jedrek*. He didn't take his eyes from the dragon. He would take care of this threat first and prove himself to Jedrek once and for all. The dragon was also distracted by Jedrek, which gave Nick the opening he needed. He leapt, and was surprised when he was slammed into from the side, a familiar scent swirling around him. He roared his displeasure, but the black beast tangling with him simply roared back, his flame-filled eyes demanding *something*. Nick snarled and was met with one in return. Jedrek was displeased with him. Nick huffed and Jedrek lowered his weight, his heavy, overheated body pressing Nick into the grass. He didn't like it and snarled once more, but Jedrek ignored him. He'd very much displeased him. It wouldn't do.

Nick tried to squirm away, howled and chuffed his protest, but Jedrek refused to budge. He wouldn't even meet Nick's gaze. Nick howled.

"Do you have him?" A feminine voice, but another scent of heat and burning.

Nick roared and tried to writhe free, but he couldn't move.

"He's got him." Another voice, this one filled with power. The big man with flaming eyes. The alpha of alphas. Then the other. The alpha of the hellhounds. Nick roared, demanding their assistance.

The woman closed her eyes and held her hands above them. Nick was embraced by more heat. He tried to burrow beneath Jedrek's form, searching for another way to escape, but none came. And then quiet. Silence in his mind. Calm in his heart. He leaned back, searching the circle of others who now surrounded him. He looked to Jedrek, who finally met his gaze as Jedrek shifted back into his human form.

Nick huffed.

"He's back," Jedrek said. "Nick, talk to me."

Nick growled and pushed his head into Jedrek's chest. Jedrek held his mane, tight the way Nick liked it.

"Okay, maybe not fully back," Jedrek said.

"Nick!"

The dragon groaned, but Nick knew that voice. He lifted his head and roared. Sawyer skidded to a stop.

"Whoa."

Nick chuffed and moved his head toward the door. Sawyer should be resting.

"Did you just tell me to go back to bed?"

Nick huffed.

"Oh my goddess, you totally did. Nick! I'm fine. I swear, you're worse than my mates."

Nick grumbled.

"You can let him go," Sawyer said. "He won't hurt me."

"Sawyer—" the dragon said.

"He's my brother," Sawyer said. He skirted around Draco and came over to Nick. "He's a pretty kitty. Yes, he is."

Nick fluffed out his mane and butted his head into Sawyer's chest. He was not a kitty.

"Oh, come on, Nick. You're so pretty. Look at you. I mean, you're totally fierce, don't get me wrong, and totally majestic. King of the jungle, and all that."

Nick chuffed. That's exactly what he was. And Sawyer shouldn't forget it.

Sawyer leaned in and wrapped his arms around Nick's neck. "I'm so glad you're able to shift again. This big guy deserves to be let out to play, you know? He's probably more than a little cranky about being locked away for so long. I think we should ask Zaire to look at the remnants of yours and Mikey's pendants from Mama Thea. Is that okay with you? I mean, now that I know... it's different. I... don't know. I want someone who understands magic more than I do to take a look at them."

"Actually," Zaire said, "I spoke to the hellhounds. They are sending Jedrek to guard my son and his coven, and I asked for Nick to come as well. I want to find out who dared to take the cubs and hurt them, and that includes your foster brother."

"My brother," Sawyer corrected. "They're my brothers."

Zaire smiled, and Nick chuffed, rubbing his head against Sawyer's chest again.

"I know, buddy. People never get it until we tell them, but that's why we just say it. Mama Thea always said that blood was thicker than water, but what we have is made of stronger stuff that that. Who needs blood when you have an unbreakable bond like ours?"

Forged in bad times, Nick's mind provided.

"Vibranium," Sawyer said. "If it's strong enough for Captain America's shield, it's strong enough for us."

Nick chuffed again. They'd let him watch way too many Marvel movies as a kid. They used to say titanium until Sawyer got into his superhero phase. And now look at him. He was probably trying to think of a code name for Nick as they stood there.

"Dude, you're totally Lionheart! I need to look him up!"

Nick huffed and bumped his head into Sawyer hard enough that he made a sound and stepped back.

"Fine. Sheesh. But what do you say? Can Zaire take the pendants? Do you want to go to her place and see if you can finally solve the mystery?"

Nick rolled his shoulders back and shifted into his human form. He knelt on the grass, gasping for breath, his chest aching and sore. "Shit, that hurts."

"What? What's wrong? Vaughn!"

"I'm fine, Sawyer."

"No, you're not fine. I've met you. If you say it hurts, it really fucking hurts."

"Nick, why don't you come inside and let me check things out? It'll make Sawyer feel better."

Nick looked up at the doctor, then at his brother's concerned expression. "Fine."

"I'm coming with you," Sawyer said. "And don't try to argue."

"You do realize I'm the big brother, right?" Nick's voice ached like he'd been screaming.

"And I'm the annoying little brother so shut up and come on."

Nick looked over his shoulder and found Jedrek watching. He nodded toward the clinic and bent down to pick up Nick's discarded clothes. Nick let Sawyer drag him into the building and toward one of the exam rooms. Both Jedrek and Draco followed, and Nick realized he felt relieved. He was afraid of the lion side of him, what it would do. He'd lost control twice. What if he hurt his brothers?

"Okay, boys, you're all waiting outside," Vaughn said. "Don't argue with me, Sawyer. Don't make me call my grandmother."

Sawyer gasped. "You'd tell Nana on me?"

"In a hot minute. Now go."

"Fine, but I want to know what's going on. And you better tell me."

"I'll tell you," Nick said. "I promise."

"Even if you think I can't handle it."

"I'll tell you. Doc, you have my permission to tell my brother whatever you find out."

Sawyer leaned against Draco. "Don't tell him something else when I go."

"I won't."

Sawyer left and the door closed softly behind him. Jedrek remained in the room, a big, hulking presence. Nick caught his gaze and couldn't look away. "Did I hurt you?"

Jedrek scoffed. "I'm more worried that I hurt you. I hit you hard. Maybe broke a rib."

Vaughn pointed to the exam table and Nick hopped up onto it. He was poked and prodded for a number of minutes before the doctor scribbled a few final notes on his clipboard and looked up with a smile. "Nothing broken. Your shifts seem to take a lot out of you. Your body is adjusting, and after so long not shifting, these are honestly slighter reactions than I would have anticipated."

"So what? Try not to shift? 'Cause I can't exactly control it."

"On the contrary, I think you should continue to shift, but try to work on changing when you want to versus when your lion demands. Daily shifting, perhaps twice daily depending on your needs. Let your lion roam free a little, but expect some general soreness when you return to your human form. I'll send along some tiger balm salve. It's great for sore muscles and should soothe the aches a bit."

"Tiger balm. Funny, Doc."

Vaughn grinned. "Have Zaire contact me if you have any worse symptoms, but I believe you'll be fine."

Taking his clipboard with him, Vaughn walked out of the exam room and closed the door softly behind him. Jedrek handed Nick his clothes, which he began to pull on.

Jedrek leaned back against the wall and drew Nick's attention as he pulled up his pants.

"What?"

"I didn't say anything."

Nick huffed.

"Going nonverbal on me again, huh?"

It was strange, this ability for Jedrek to read him so well. With Sawyer and Mikey, they demanded that he talk. He hated trying to put everything he felt into words. Nick just looked at him.

"I'm normally the quiet one, so this is weird for me."

Jedrek had done nothing but talk since the moment they met. Nick liked hearing him talk, actually.

"So you heard Zaire. She wants you to come to hers so she can help figure out what they did to you guys. I think it's a good idea. My alpha is sending me, too, since she's also pissed that we brought her son into our big fight earlier. I'll tell you about it later. Keziah's really powerful, though, and he's in a really strong coven."

"You think they can help me?"

"I do."

Nick nodded. "I lost it a bit."

"Sounded like it. But you brought it back fast."

Only because Jedrek had tackled him. He'd wanted to take a chunk out of Draco's hide. "I don't want to hurt anyone."

"So we'll work on your control. That's what the doc said you needed." Jedrek looked toward the door moments before someone knocked on it. "It's Zaire."

Nick inhaled and caught a hint of her scent. "Come in."

She opened the door and looked him over. "You look better."

Nick shrugged.

"I wanted to speak to you before, but now will do. I want to catch those fuckers who hurt you and the others. I want it more than the very air I breathe. But for the grace of the goddess, that could have been my son."

"And you need my help to do it?"

"We haven't had any leads in years. I can taste their magic now, more clearly than ever. This is the chance we needed."

Nick glanced at Jedrek, who simply gave him a blank look in return. It was his call, his choice. He wanted to find them as much as Zaire did, wanted them to pay, but he had other concerns now. Mainly his brothers. He couldn't leave them unprotected. If they were attacked again, Nick wanted to be there.

"I can get you back here through a portal," Jedrek said. "Fast. The moment we get a call."

"But those are the only circumstances in which you will be portaling in and out of my home," Zaire warned. "I will not let you put me and mine in danger. The threat is too real to ignore."

Both Sawyer and Mikey had their mates, and with the wards, Nick could at least get notice. The chance to find the magic users responsible had been his quest his entire life. He couldn't mess up the chance to find them. "Okay, I'll help you."

"Excellent. I took the liberty of having Cecil gather some of your things. We need to go. I want to get to work."

It took Nick a second to process. "What do you mean... gather some of my—"

"Clothes and stuff." Zaire snapped her fingers at him, and then glared at Jedrek. "Let's go."

She turned and went down the hall.

"Did she just..."

"Yep," Jedrek said.

"It's best not to question her. Go talk to your brother. He's worried. I'll stall her for another couple minutes."

Nick hopped off the exam table and stopped to breathe deeply. He choked on the heavy scent of antiseptic, but then he found Jedrek's scent. Heat, warmth, flame. He wanted to curl up around it. The lion in him loved heat. Hot desert days. He was built for heat. He opened his eyes, not realizing he'd even closed them, and found Jedrek's flame-filled gaze on him. He definitely fit the bill; hot was an understatement.

He moved closer, drawn to that scent. The closer he came, the more he felt. Heat, warmth, longing, desire, anticipation.

"Nick—"

Jedrek felt it, too. He could see it in his eyes now, smell it in the subtle changes of his scent. His lion crept forward, not taking charge this time, but simply informing him. There. That one. That means he wants you too. And that, that one. That means he's yours.

Nick touched Jedrek's side, just under his ribs. Close to his vulnerable belly, but not too close. No, he didn't want to spook him. He moved closer, slid his hand around to Jedrek's back. The man was a giant, even if his alphas stood taller. He had weight to him, solidity. He wasn't going anywhere. Nick liked it. He couldn't be broken. He leaned in, tucked his nose against Jedrek's neck and breathed.

"Fuck," Jedrek groaned. "This is not the time, Nick."

"I know," Nick replied. But he couldn't resist one little taste. He nipped at Jedrek's neck and flavor burst across his tongue.

Jedrek's hands gripped his hips, and Nick all but purred at the touch.

"Go see your brother."

"I will. But this isn't over. Is it?"

Jedrek sucked in a breath and his hands tightened. "No. It isn't."

Nick leaned back and met Jedrek's gaze, then leaned in again. "Good."

He backed away, not because he wanted to, but because he knew someone would be in checking on them. He didn't want them interrupted. He went down the hall to the room where his brothers were. Sawyer stood when he entered and sighed after looking at him. "You're going."

"Yes, Doc says I'm fine. Just need to practice shifting," Nick said. "But if anything happens, Jedrek and I will come. He promised he'd bring me right away."

"Find who did this to you," Sawyer said. He glanced down at Mikey's still form, then back to Nick. "Mikey would want you to find them, too."

"I will."

Sawyer wrapped him in a hug and squeezed tight. Nick returned it. Before Sawyer let him go, he looked up, clenching his fists in Nick's shirt. "And Nick?"

"Yeah?"

"Get in a good hit for Henry."

Nick grinned at the fierce anger and protectiveness in his brother's eyes. There was the tough kid he knew. "They'll regret the day they crossed us, little brother."

Sawyer nodded and let him go. Nick touched Mikey's leg, and sent a glance to his mates. They both nodded to him, seeming to approve of his departure as well. They understood, and they would explain it to Mikey should he wake and Nick not be there. "Let me know if there are any changes."

"We will," Asher said.

"Go," Sawyer said. "And keep your damn phone with you. And answer my damn calls."

"Yeah, yeah," Nick said. "Be safe and no fighting with gods. Or goddesses. Whatever. You hear me?"

Sawyer grinned. "I'll do my best."

Nick let him go and went for the door. Draco stood on the other side. "You better keep him safe."

"I will. Find who hurt Henry," Draco said softly. "And call me when you do. I wouldn't mind helping."

Nick grinned and clapped him on the shoulder before leaving the clinic. Jedrek stood outside holding two stuffed bags, an old, familiar, battered suitcase, and oddly, what appeared to be a donut box.

"Zaire got tired of waiting. She took Leandra and her cubs on and we're to meet her there."

"I have no idea who they are," Nick said.

"Oh, right. Come on, I'll tell you when we get there." Jedrek opened a portal and stepped through. Nick took one last glance at the clinic and the shifters guarding his brothers standing near the door, then he followed Jedrek through. They emerged in a patch of woods, standing within a circle of stones.

"What the hell?"

"Zaire's paranoid. She doesn't allow portals inside her wards. We have to wait here until she comes back for us."

Nick reached out his hand and got a nice zap when he tried to reach across the stones. His lion did not approve.

"So, Leandra. Her kids were part of what happened to you as well. From what we could find out from her, someone used some sort of magic on her and she ended up pregnant."

"She was raped."

"That's where it's a little murky. We're not sure sex was involved, but magic was absolutely used on her against her will so I have no issues using that word. The weird thing is, we aren't sure there are fathers involved. We're trying to figure out how it happened, though, and if someone is able to make like the Virgin Mary and get impregnated."

Nick scowled and circled the stones. "So there's a possibility that we were all 'virgin' births, as it were."

"I don't know. I doubt it. Leandra is the first mother we've found, and none of you guys seem to recall being around your mothers. If whoever is doing this doesn't give a shit about the mothers, I don't think they give a shit as to how they get them pregnant. The kids seem to be the goal."

"They messed with our magic," Nick said. "Messed with my magic, and the others."

Jedrek nodded.

"And probably killed our mothers."

Jedrek nodded.

"We need to kill these bastards."

"We could do that," Jedrek said. "Or we could take them to hell and let my goddess deal with it. She's a lot more creative, and she definitely won't end it for them fast."

Nick's lion itched beneath his skin, but he pushed him gently back. He didn't want to change again so soon. He wanted to think it through, process with his human brain what he knew. The sooner they had answers, the better he'd feel.

JEDREK

Zaire hadn't left them waiting long, but it was enough to put Nick on edge. She took one look at him pacing and freed them from the wards. She led them directly toward her home. Except it wasn't the hippie fest commune Jedrek had been expecting. It looked like a subdivision. Well, one street of one, anyway. Like that House-wife show Calli'd been addicted to, even though she'd pretended like she wasn't. A dozen or so houses, all with trimmed hedges and shiny windows.

Everything looked perfect, too perfect.

Jedrek shivered. Cul de sacs gave him the creeps.

"What's wrong?" Nick asked softly.

"Nothing. Everything's fine."

Nick scowled but turned his attention back to Zaire. She stopped in front of a little, one-story house that might as well have had a white picket fence and a golden retriever in the yard. She pushed open the door and gestured them inside.

"I've put you both here. I hope you don't mind sharing, but with Izzy and Sophie, and now Leandra and the kids, I'm running low on guest accommodations."

"What the hell is this place?"

"My home," Zaire said her voice icy. "I'd like for you to stay in tonight and get settled. There's food in the freezer, but if you need anything, just make a list and I'll have it taken care of. I need to let our other residents know that a hellhound is here."

"Sure," Jedrek said.

She gave them both stern looks before turning and leaving again. Jedrek looked around the place. It was nice, but not extravagant. Off-white walls, crisp white trim. Hardwood floors. A nice woven rug. Perfectly serviceable couch. Dear goddess, he'd been banished to suburbia. He'd obviously done something horrific to deserve this level of punishment.

"Could this place be any more boring if it tried?" Nick asked. "I feel like I'm trapped in one of those model homes."

Jedrek huffed and dropped the bags and Nick's suitcase. He needed a donut. The kitchen was at the other end of the room, tucked behind a bookcase that had two books and a lot of knickknacks, including a white hand. Why did anyone need a sculpture of a hand sitting on their bookshelf? Or one of those fake lumps of coral? He sighed and found a roll of paper towels tucked away under the sink. Nick had followed him so he tore off two before opening the box and giving Nick first dibs.

"We're living in a catalog," Jedrek grumbled. He found one of the chocolate ones with sprinkles and grabbed it.

"I mean, it's nice and all," Nick hedged. "It's better than my place."

"At least it has furniture."

Nick snorted and took a bite of a powdered sugar donut. It left a ring of white around his lips. Jedrek kind of wanted to lick it off for him.

"I have furniture," Nick protested.

"Sure you do. You know what I never got about those fancy shows where they fix up the houses?"

"What?" Nick asked between bites.

"Where do they put their stuff? I mean, it doesn't make sense. They give 'em like one shelf, and it's perfectly styled or whatever, but where do you put your remotes? And your mail? Or just your stuff. Books and magazines and the picture your kids paint for you at school."

"Have kids, do you?"

Jedrek glared. "I have kids in my life. Well, had kids. The Jerrick kids don't exactly do crafts anymore. Still have Sophie, though. Can't wait to see the little munchkin."

"Who's Sophie?"

"Izzy's a waitress at the bar we run. She's human, but part of our pack. Sophie's her six-year-old daughter. Izzy found out about all this because someone used magic and sent her ex after her. It was too dangerous so Meshaq sent her here to keep her and Sophie safe."

Nick finished his donut and licked his fingers. "Let's see what else this place has."

Jedrek took the last bite of his and followed Nick down the only hall in the place. There were two bedrooms and a shared bathroom between them. It was basically a step up from the cabins at the clinic. "I'll take this one, if you don't care."

Nick turned and was suddenly in Jedrek's space. "I don't care."

His husky voice made his intentions abundantly clear.

"Nick," Jedrek groaned.

"We've got time to kill. And I have a few ideas of how to spend that time."

"This isn't—"

"I know. It's a terrible idea. Really. One of my worst. But I want to taste you. I want to see your skin. I want to spread you out and take you apart. My instincts are going crazy. You smell so fucking good."

Nick leaned in and Jedrek should have pulled away but he didn't. He let Nick get close, press him back against the bedroom wall, and bury his face in Jedrek's neck. Nick touched him, his hands on

Jedrek's arms, squeezing, testing their strength before he drifted up and over his shoulders. All while his wicked mouth worked on Jedrek's neck, tasting him. Marking him.

"Fuck," Jedrek groaned.

"That's what I'm hoping," Nick rumbled.

His voice deepened. He lifted his head and stared into Jedrek's eyes. The golden glow of the lion stared back, but Nick was still in control. Jedrek's eyes flared in return.

Jedrek threw caution to the wind and grabbed his shirt. He pulled it off before grabbing Nick's face in his hands. He hesitated for only a second before diving in and getting his first taste of the man.

Everything stopped. The heat between them burst into flame, an inferno of aching want that shot straight to Jedrek's cock. It thickened and he thrust forward, pushing into Nick only to find answering hardness.

Nick's eyes brightened, turning a pure golden yellow as he pulled back and pulled his own shirt over his head. "Get on the bed."

His voice had bottomed out, deep with lust and power. Jedrek trembled. Goddess, he loved a man who was his equal, who could take what he gave and then give it right back in return. Nothing about Nick was fragile. Everything about him radiated power and lust.

Jedrek walked backward to the bed, pushing his pants down as he went. By the time he reached the mattress, he was gloriously naked, his skin golden and beaded with sweat. "Lube is in my bag," Jedrek said.

Nick growled, pausing mid-step before spinning around and going back into the living room. Jedrek stroked his cock then spread his legs, teasing his balls, getting himself nice and hard.

A low growl pulled his attention back to the doorway. Nick moved slowly, a predator hunting his prey. He never took his eyes of Jedrek's dick, captivated by each slow, sensuous movement of Jedrek's hand. He dropped the lube and condoms on the side table before climbing onto the bed. He had his hands on either side of

Jedrek's hips, his eyes still locked on Jedrek's hand as it moved in a slow steady rhythm.

Nick slowly lowered his head and the predatory gleam in his eye sent a shiver down Jedrek's spine. He'd fucked a lot, but he'd never had anyone look at him like this. Nick kept his eyes on Jedrek's hand but breathed against his balls. He reflexively tightened them and Nick looked up, grinning before he opened his mouth and sucked one into his mouth.

Jedrek groaned at the wet heat. Nick rumbled and the vibrations sent another tremble through him. He stopped stroking his cock, because he could already feel the dam of pleasure building in his spine, and it would burst way too soon if he didn't. Nick didn't seem to appreciate his efforts at control, though. He glared and released the ball in his mouth, licked a stripe up the other, then moved upward.

"Nick," Jedrek groaned.

Nick took his eyes from his prize and looked up. "So fucking hot."

"I'm kinda on edge here, man."

"Then let's take the edge off."

His voice deepened so much Jedrek hardly recognized it. He had Jedrek's dick in his hand then, squeezing and stroking, getting a feel for it. It was enough to increase that pressure he'd tried to hold back tenfold. It didn't seem to matter. Nick wanted it. He leaned in and sucked the tip between his lips, laving at the slit and the come that gathered there. Jedrek groaned and his hips pushed up, an instinct he couldn't fight if he tried. Nick grinned wickedly, then lowered his head further.

"Fuck," Jedrek yelled.

Nick sucked him deeper, the heat and warmth sending sparks through his body. Jedrek tried to hold back, but it was a lost cause. He'd never been worked up so fast, so desperate to come that he didn't want to stretch it out. He tried. He fought it. Letting the exquisite pressure build until Nick brushed a finger against his hole, and the promise in the gesture sent him over the edge. Nick hummed against him as he began to thrust desperately, come shooting into Nick's mouth as he continued to work him over.

When he finally finished, Nick raised his head and visibly swallowed.

Then he licked his lips and the wicked grin was back. "My turn."

He crawled forward, legs straddling Jedrek's waist, then his chest. Jedrek's breath heaved, still gasping from the pleasure at his orgasm. But heat already began to build again at the promise. Nick grabbed the headboard and looked down at him. His eyes made the demand, and Jedrek was all too happy to comply. He scooted down and opened his mouth. Nick used one hand to feed Jedrek his cock while the other braced against the headboard.

"That's it. Fuck, Jed. You're so fucking hot. That mouth of yours. I've been thinking of it. Imagining you on your knees with my cock in the back of your throat."

Jedrek growled again, licking and slurping at everything Nick gave him. He could feel it when it became too much, when Nick started to lose control. His thighs tightened, squeezing against Jedrek's shoulders. His cock twitched in his mouth. His head dropped and he clenched the headboard tighter.

And then he came, come hitting the back of Jedrek's throat. He pulled out, shooting across Jedrek's neck and the top of his chest. His eyes glowed, bright golden yellow as he orgasmed. The lion took control, his instincts guiding Nick as he rubbed his come into Jedrek's skin, scenting him. Marking his territory. Jedrek didn't mind at all. He panted for breath, mouth still watering. Wanting more. Nick's cock didn't even soften, and Jedrek realized his own hadn't either. He'd been so focused on Nick he hadn't realized he'd gotten wound up again. Of course, now that he was aware of it, he wanted Nick's hands back on him. Or his mouth. Or both.

Nick seemed inclined to agree. He slowly moved back down, straddling Jedrek's waist and using his shoulders for support. He had him pinned to the mattress. Jedrek grabbed Nick's hips, pushing him down just that little bit further so their cocks sat next to each other. Nick liked the idea. He began to slowly roll his hips, thrusting his cock next to Jedrek's.

"Look what you do to me," Nick rumbled. "So fucking turned on, I'm ready to go again. That's never happened before. Only you. So fucking hot."

Nick slid his hands down and grabbed Jedrek's pecs. He squeeze, then leaned down and bit, not hard but enough for Jedrek to feel it all the way to his toes. "Nick."

"Yeah. Gonna mark you up." He moved to the other side and laved Jedrek's nipple with his tongue. He bit down on it, softly tugging it between his teeth before releasing it.

He moved further down, his mouth ghosting over Jedrek's ribs, and then down to his hip. He sucked another mark there. Down further, spreading Jedrek's legs. He nipped at his thigh, then sucked a mark. Down further, to his calf, and then at his ankle.

Bright golden eyes looked up at him. "Turn over."

"Nick."

He got a growl in return. The sound about sent him over the edge. He rolled over, spread his legs and arms, offered himself up to Nick.

"Hmm," Nick groaned.

He traced his lips over Jedrek's calf, to the sensitive spot behind his knee. He moved to the other side, sucked a mark on Jedrek's thigh. Both hands grabbed his ass, kneading him, spreading him open. Hot breath against his hole and then then rumbling of Nick's voice. "I'll come back for you."

Then up. The dip in his back. Beneath his shoulder blade. And finally, his neck. Jedrek shivered. "Nick."

"Hmm."

Nick's weight moved slightly to the side but was quickly back again. He heard the snick of the lube bottle, then the cool liquid hitting the crease of his ass. Nick's fingers followed, traced his hole, then he pushed two inside. Jedrek tensed, his body arching back. Nick seemed a master of his body already, instinctively knowing where to touch, where he needed it. He thrust hard and fast. Then added another. All the while he breathed on Jedrek's neck, the most sensitive, most sacred spot of him. But Nick seemed to know that too. He bit down gently and Jedrek cried out. His hole ached, wanted more so badly.

Nick reached for the condoms. Tore one off. Then cursed.

"What?"

"Tore it. Hold on."

"Don't need it," Jedrek confessed.

Nick stilled. "What?"

"Can't get anything. Hellhound."

Nick's breathing deepened and he moved his lips up further to Jedrek's ear. "You sure?"

"Yes. Please, Nick. I need you."

Those seemed to be the words he needed to hear. He added lube to his cock, forced Jedrek's legs wider, then pushed his cock against Jedrek's hole. It was big, bigger than he'd been prepared for and they both knew it. But Nick, fucking hell, Nick knew exactly what he was doing. He eased his way inside, slowly stretching him.

His mouth was back at Jedrek's neck, teasing, driving him insane with need. But he couldn't even move. Not in this position. Nick had him spread out and even when he tried to move his hips, to get some friction against his achingly hard cock, he couldn't. He could barely move. Nick had him, though.

"Arch your back," Nick rumbled.

He had to comply. Jedrek arched, pushing his hips up, changing the angle. Nick slid deeper, a rumbling growl in his ear. "You were made for me, for this. You're sucking me in now, aren't you? Perfect ass, Jed. So fucking perfect. Think you can take me? Can you take it all?"

Jedrek groaned again. Like he could form words at the moment. He couldn't think past the sensations, the sparks of pleasure spiraling through his body. But he did it anyway, forced his body to relax, and it had the desired result. Nick bottomed out, his dick fully buried in Jedrek's ass. He got another grumble for his effort, this one pleased. Nick's mouth was back at his neck. He added another mark as he slowly rolled his hips. Desire ratcheted up with each brush of Nick's cock against the bundle of nerves inside him.

But Nick wasn't going to be rushed. He wasn't going to let Jedrek decide how this went. It turned him on further. And he relaxed into the mattress, even though his cock ached now. Wanting his hand on it. It would only take a few pulls and it would be over again. But Jedrek didn't want it to be over.

Nick's rhythm changed, becoming a sharp staccato punch. His breathing quickened, becoming more desperate. Jedrek knew the feeling. Heat built between them, waves of it pouring off Jedrek to Nick, and then back again.

"Nick."

"Fuck yeah," Nick said. "So fucking hot, Jed. You're burning me up. Fuck."

His rhythm faltered, and the change was enough to shove Jedrek off the edge. One last thrust pegged his gland and he threw back his head. He yelled Nick's name as his orgasm struck, his hole tightening, trapping Nick's dick exactly where he wanted it. Nick didn't seem to mind. With his head back and throat exposed, Nick grabbed him and bit down. Hard. And his hot come filled Jedrek's ass.

Jedrek collapsed onto the mattress. Stunned. He'd... shit. He'd let Nick claim him.

"Mmm," Nick released his hold and rolled his softening cock around once more before pulling free. He slid to the side, curling himself around Jedrek's side and tucking his face into Jedrek's neck. "So good."

And yeah. Yeah it was.

Nick stroked his back, his big hand dragging down Jedrek's spine, dipping into the crease and the dripping mess he'd left behind. Nick didn't care. He simply kept touching, learning, exploring. Jedrek relaxed into it. Nothing he could do to change things now, and he'd never had this. Never had someone so entranced with his body. With him. He sighed, but it turned into a yawn.

"Sleep," Nick murmured quietly against his neck. "I've got you."

So Jedrek closed his eyes and did as he was told.

NICK

Nick *felt* more than smelled someone approaching the house. He peeled open one eye and breathed deeply, cocking a grin at the scent of a well-fucked man next to him. Jedrek hadn't moved, but lay face down on the bed, his legs spread enough for Nick to have one thigh tucked between them. He'd found a spot he liked against Jedrek's side, half on him, half off. Jedrek's shoulder served as a makeshift pillow. Nick hadn't slept so well in years.

Footsteps outside grew closer and Nick fought back a growl. He rolled to the side and sucked in another breath, this one reminding himself what Zaire would do to him if he didn't stay in control. Jedrek grumbled but didn't wake. Nick paused one more moment to take in the view before moving quickly toward the front door. He opened it just in time. The guy on the porch had his hand raised to knock.

"Who are you?" Nick said. His voice was low and growly. He might have roared a bit loudly the night before. He wanted to go back to bed and roar a little more.

The guy looked at Nick, then down, then blushed, then back up again. "I'm, um. Wow. Uh. See, there's... uh, what's my name?"

Nick looked down, realized he was stark naked and filthy. Sticky and covered in come. *Nice.* He ran his hand down his belly and made a little rumbling sound of approval.

"Right. Um, I'm Rowan. That's my name. Oh, goddess."

"What do you want, Rowan?"

"Well..." Rowan looked Nick up and down once more and Nick was pretty sure he might pass out if he turned any redder.

"Who is it?" Jedrek grumbled behind him. He came up and tugged Nick back against him, tucking his face into Nick's neck.

"Some guy."

"Go put pants on. He's gonna faint."

"Oh, hi Jedrek."

Nick scowled. "You know this guy?"

Jedrek lifted his head and peeled open his eyes. "Yeah. That's Rowan. Come back to bed."

"Um, Zaire wanted you guys to come up to her place. She sent me to get you."

Nick growled, and the guy stepped back.

"You could shower first. That's probably b-best," Rowan stuttered.

Jedrek chuckled. "Yeah. Give us a few minutes."

Jedrek tugged Nick back and shut the door in Rowan's face.

"You shocked him," Jedrek said. "And showed him your cock. I thought I said that was mine."

"Did you?" Nick said. He turned and pressed their bodies together. He wanted again, which he didn't think possible. They'd fucked for hours, passed out a while, then fucked some more. But he couldn't get enough.

"Shower. Zaire won't like it if we keep her waiting."

Nick nipped at Jedrek's neck in protest, but let himself be lead toward the bathroom. Jedrek pushed him back once they were in the room and growled at him.

Nick grinned and cupped Jedrek's ass in one hand, giving the muscled globe a squeeze. "What?"

"Shower."

Jedrek pulled away and opened the glass shower door before turning on the water. He waited for it to heat up, holding his hand under as a test, then pointed.

"Fine," Nick said. "You joining me?"

"No, because I can't keep my hands off you. But hurry up. Rowan's waiting."

Nick scowled as Jedrek left the room, but he got in the shower anyway. He wanted to talk to Zaire again, to find out what the plan was for tracking down the magic users. It was just that he wanted to fuck Jedrek again first.

He sniffed the provided bottle of shower gel and scowled at its natural herbiness. He squirted some on his palm anyway before smoothing it over his body, getting rid of the sticky remains of lube and cum that stuck to him. Jedrek came back in the room with a stack of clothes and a toiletries bag in his hand.

"You done?"

"No."

Jedrek sighed and pulled out his toothbrush and toothpaste. He started brushing, but didn't look away, watching as Nick continued his shower behind the glass door. A toothbrush had never looked so suggestive, sliding in and out of Jedrek's mouth.

He leaned over the sink and spit out the foamy toothpaste, which itself was some sort of sign, bending over. His ass just right there...

"Stop," Jedrek groaned. "This is *not* sexy."

But Nick begged to differ. He opened the shower door but didn't have to step out. Jedrek was right there, hands gripping his hips tight. Then devouring his mouth with his minty-fresh glory.

Jedrek stepped beneath the water, moving Nick back as they kissed, but then he pushed him away again. "You're too tempting."

Nick huffed and went for Jedrek's neck again, but a hand on his chest stopped him. "After."

As much as he wanted to protest, Jedrek was right. He got out of the shower, refusing to look back. After grabbing a towel, he wrapped it around his hips and made his way into the living room where they'd abandoned his suitcase the night before. He was surprised as hell to find that it contained more than his clothes. His entire wall of research had been dismantled and packed up, tucked neatly in a folder. He had a fair amount of clothes— including his boxer briefs, neatly folded which he never did— and his charger for his phone.

Nick grabbed a change of clothes— it was so weird having everything neatly folded, and strangely unwrinkled. He couldn't ever remember seeing his T-shirts unwrinkled— and returned to the bathroom with the folder in one hand and his clothes in the other.

Jedrek was rinsing off and, not being a crazy man, Nick paused and enjoyed the view. When the water turned off, Nick sighed, sad the show was over, and began drying off the rest of the way so he could pull his clothes on.

"What's that?" Jedrek asked.

He'd wisely stayed in the shower, although he'd opened the door and grabbed a towel. Damn, the man was so beautiful, Nick wanted to—

"Nick?"

"Sorry. It's my notes from my research wall. They were in my suitcase. I thought, I don't know, maybe Zaire would want to see them."

"That's a good idea."

Jedrek stepped out and grabbed his clothes, but not without sending a heated look Nick's way.

"See, not just me, is it?"

"Fuck no," Jedrek said. "But also, Zaire might curse us."

Nick tugged his shirt over his head and slapped some toothpaste on his toothbrush. He made sure to be as obscene as possible in his brushing, even as Jedrek laughed and ignored him as he got dressed.

He liked the sound. A lot. Damn, he felt good. Better than he had in... ever. He'd never felt this good. So rested and just... calm. Chill. 'Course, he'd never had such amazing sex before either. He was pretty sure that had a lot to do with it. He grinned and spit before wiping his face and running his fingers through his wet hair. "Good enough?"

Jedrek pressed up behind him and their eyes met in the mirror. "To eat." Nick pressed back into him, but another knock sounded on the front door. Jedrek sighed and smacked Nick's ass. "Let's go."

Nick shoved his feet into a pair of flip flops from his bag. He really needed to remember to ask just who had packed for him. Rowan looked sheepish when Jedrek pulled open the door. "Uh, sorry to bother you but Zaire is really antsy."

"We're coming," Jedrek said.

Rowan glanced down, as if he thought Jedrek might actually be coming at that exact moment, and immediately blushed. Nick snorted out a laugh. "That's a filthy mind you've got there, Rowan."

Nick was pretty sure the poor guy's face was going to burst into flames.

"N-not usually. It's just—" Rowan waved his arm around.

"I get it. He's hot like burning. It's a hellhound thing. But don't worry. I already took care of the coming part this morning. You don't have to worry about that."

"So smug. Such a lion thing," Jedrek said. He ran his hand up Nick's belly, pulling up his T-shirt to reveal his abs. Rowan gulped and backed up, but he was too close to the stairs and tripped.

Nick didn't know he could move so fast, but he managed to catch Rowan and ended up with the poor guy cradled in his arms.

Jedrek cackled. The ass.

"You know, you're supposedly faster than me. Why didn't you catch him?"

"Hey," Jedrek protested. "I could have caught him."

"Um, could you maybe put me down?"

"Then why didn't you?" Nick asked. "Because you were too slow. Admit it."

Jedrek grabbed the folder Nick had dropped in his haste to catch Rowan and walked off the porch. "Faster than you."

Nick followed him. "Sure you are. I believe the proof is right here." He lifted the guy, who really didn't weigh much at all, as proof of his winning status.

"I let you get him. You clearly were trying to impress me. Color me impressed."

"Impress you? I still needed to impress you? I'm pretty sure I impressed you a lot last night. And this morning. And—"

"Point," Jedrek said. "Which way?"

Rowan had his hand over his face, which was still unnaturally red. "If he puts me down, I can show you."

"You sure you're okay to walk? You seem a little shaky."

"Goddess save me," Rowan groaned.

Nick smirked at Jedrek, who met his grin. He put the guy down, and Jedrek grabbed Nick's arm, pulling him close.

"My hero," he grumbled, before he nipped at Nick's neck.

"That's what I want to hear," Nick said. He patted Jedrek's ass and gave him a little more room to work.

"Uh, guys? *Zaire?* Can we, uh, go?"

Jedrek pulled away and sighed. "You should plan on impressing me again later."

"Duly noted."

Nick and Jedrek followed Rowan, who hadn't stopped blushing, down the street toward one of the larger houses. Nick really didn't have any expectations for the place, but Jedrek seemed stunned. He kept looking around, shaking his head, and Nick had no doubt he had pictured something completely different.

It was a nice neighborhood, though. The houses were close, but had enough room between so they weren't on top of each other. There were a lot of trees, but Nick could see garden areas around each of the houses. There were probably a dozen or so places on the street, all built around the house they were walking toward.

Rowan gave a cursory knock on the door before he pushed it open. Inside, a much different looking Zaire sat in an oversized chair with a young man at her side who had to be her son. They were both stunning to look at, but where Zaire had seemed ferocious the last time they saw her, she looked weak now.

Jedrek rushed forward and knelt by her chair. "What happened?"

Rowan carried in a really foul smelling bowl of something or other and handed it to her. "Thank you, Rowan. Will you see if our guests need anything?"

"Sure."

But before he could ask, Jedrek's eyes flared. "Zaire!"

"I'll be fine."

"Mom, you're not fine."

"Keziah, what happened?"

He glanced at his mother once more before turning his attention to Jedrek. "She tried to untangle the magic from the ward on her own. She knows better."

"And she's sitting right here and doesn't appreciate the tone."

Jedrek growled. "Dumb ass move, Zaire."

"You should have called your coven together. You'd skin me if I thought about tackling something like that without my coven's support."

Zaire scoffed, but she tightened her hold on Keziah's hand.

Nick didn't know a thing about all this magic everyone kept talking about. Wards and portals and covens. He'd thought being a shifter was the most abnormal thing around. Of course, knowing his brother was a god was now top of his list of weirdest shit on the planet.

"Hey, are aliens real?" Nick asked.

Four sets of eyes turned to him, equally stunned. Zaire cackled and pointed to the sofa beside her.

"Nick, I think you've learned enough of the world's mysteries for one day. Have a seat."

Rowan disappeared into the kitchen and returned with glasses of ice water. Berries floated in the mix and Nick eyed them suspiciously before taking a sip.

Zaire and Jedrek seemed to be having a conversation of their own, mostly with glares and flashing eyes. The flashing eyes were all Jedrek. Whatever she'd done to herself had pissed his hellhound off. He liked seeing the fire in him. Made Nick want to find a reason for them to fight so they could make up.

"Dear goddess, he's horny again," Rowan groaned.

Zaire turned her attention to the young man before glancing once more to Nick. "Excuse my young friend. He's clearly never been around a newly mated pair before."

Jedrek coughed and turned as red as Rowan had been.

Nick didn't really understand. The word mates and mated had been thrown about a lot over the past day. His brothers both had mates. And if mated meant fucked like bunnies, then sure, he and Jedrek had mated.

His lion rumbled to life, protesting Nick's thoughts. He narrowed his gaze on the hellhound. "Someone care to explain to me exactly what's going on?"

Zaire's eyes widened and Keziah began coughing, having apparently choked on his own spit. Rowan blushed again, and Jedrek... well, Jedrek just sat there stunned.

"Did you, or did you not, bite the back of his neck?" Zaire asked.

"Well, yeah," Nick said. "It was a heat of the moment kind of thing."

"Indeed," Zaire said. She turned her expression to Jedrek, who looked sheepish.

"He didn't know what he was doing."

"That doesn't change anything."

Nick growled. "What?"

"You claimed Jedrek as your mate."

Keziah finally stopped choking to death. "Or, as Cody put it, you got hellhound married."

Zaire smacked her son on the back of the head and he stared at her mutinously. "Ma! I'm not twelve."

"No, but you're acting like it. Behave. Show some respect. Nick wasn't raised in our world and has shown incredible strength and control considering the circumstances. He has just done something which cannot be undone, and yet you laugh as if it is a joke."

Keziah and Rowan both looked stunned, and Nick felt his control beginning to slip. But where he'd looked to Jedrek before for help, now he didn't know which way to turn.

"No, no. Nick. Look at me." Jedrek landed on the floor in front of him, sliding the last few inches on his knees. "You didn't do anything I didn't want you to do. And yeah, I wish you'd understood what you were doing, but you didn't do anything wrong."

"Jed," Nick growled.

"Outside," Zaire snapped.

Jedrek leapt to his feet and pulled Nick up behind him. They were on the porch within seconds.

"Nick, hold it, for a moment. Take your time. Undress. You can make it for another minute," Jedrek said.

"You have the control, Nick, use it," Zaire added.

Nick breathed even as he felt the lion demanding to be free. He pulled his shirt off, fighting back the urge to just let go. He stripped off his pants, kicking them to the side, and let out another roar. Then the lion was free. He bounded down the steps and ran, but he hadn't gone more than a dozen steps when he felt Jedrek's presence at his side.

The hellhound towered over him, but he didn't out pace him, even though Nick understood that he could. No, they ran together, until Nick reached the end of the road and a closed gate. He turned, and ran along a fence which disappeared into a grove of trees. It didn't matter. He ran, following the line of the fence with Jedrek at his side until he finally slowed, his heart beating fast and eager for a chase that wasn't presenting itself.

Jedrek waited, pacing, sniffing the air. Protecting him, Nick realized. He glanced around, recognizing magic in the air. More wards. He called to his human side and shifted back.

This time, it was Jedrek who remained in his animal form. Watching. Waiting.

"You shouldn't have let me do it," Nick said. "You should have stopped me."

Jedrek huffed and steam came out of his nose. He approached and head-butted Nick in the chest.

"Ow."

Jedrek huffed again, clearly annoyed with him.

"Fine. But don't act like you can't just shift back and talk to me like a grown up. Or human? Shit. You know, everything I say now doesn't quite make sense anymore. My whole world has— see? I was going to say shifted, but now that word means something else, too."

Jedrek tucked his head under Nick's hand, and he couldn't resist the urge to run his hand over the dark fur covering Jedrek's head.

"You just want to be petted. Giant puppy."

Jedrek huffed, but this one sounded more like a laugh.

"And this is how you understand me when I'm shifted. I get it. I understand you, too."

Using his head as a guide, Jedrek began to herd Nick backward until he bumped up against a tree. He looked up at Nick, waiting. With a sigh, Nick looked down. "Look, I think I see what you're getting at, and you're cute and a little scary all at once like this, but I'm not putting my bare ass on tree roots. You aren't that cute."

Jedrek huffed, and a second later, the man stood where the beast had been. Jedrek stripped off his shirt and tossed it in Nick's face, and then seconds later he was back in his shifted form.

"No fair," Nick groaned. But he put the shirt down and sat down anyway. Jedrek sprawled across his lap. "Why didn't you just stay human and talk to me? Also, why do I have to strip and you don't?"

Jedrek rolled over and bared his belly. Nick scratched it, accepting it for the sign of trust it was. His lion purred inside him, happy with the display.

"Okay, so you aren't mad at me. You should be. I saw the looks on their faces. What I did was serious business, right? Hellhound married? Because I bit you on the neck? I mean, look, I'm not going to lie to you, in that moment? You were totally mine and we both knew it. And I didn't know what it meant, but... I mean, damn. I've never felt like that before, you know?"

Jedrek didn't make any sounds but Nick continued to stroke his chest and stomach in long, slow passes of his hand. "You felt it, too. Look at me."

Jedrek made a little sound and hid his face behind one giant paw.

"Jedrek. Look at me."

One glowing red eye peeked out. "You feel guilty, don't you? Like you're the one who should feel bad about this and not me? How the hell does that make sense? I bit you, not the other way around. And I would have bitten you again, too. Probably this morning if we hadn't been so rudely interrupted. I mean, fuck, it felt good, you know?"

Jedrek rolled over and put his head into Nick's stomach.

"But you're thinking you shouldn't have fucked around with me because I didn't know what the deal was. Yeah, I get that, but let's face it, I wasn't in the mood for conversation last night, and yeah, I might not have done it if I'd known because I'm not exactly in control of this thing yet, and that's not the best way to... be. I'm not mad at you, though. So there's that. I just think it's crazy that we're mated or whatever and we don't know each other. I mean, I always kinda figured I'd find somebody someday and I hoped I would just know. And that's sort of the way I feel. I mean, you're so fucking hot, and I trust you. Which is weird. Because I don't trust people. Only my brothers. You can ask them."

Jedrek didn't reply, just laid against Nick for a long minute. The silence stretched and eventually, Jedrek rolled to the side and shifted back to his human form.

"I trust you, too."

And that seemed to be all he wanted to say on the matter. Jedrek looked at him, really searched his face for a long and nearly uncomfortable minute. Nick let him, though. It seemed important, and Nick tried to let his face say the words he wanted. He was confused, not mad. So attracted, but not sure why his instincts were so loud where

Jedrek was concerned. Whatever Jedrek saw, it seemed to settle something in him.

"Let's go back and check on Zaire."

Nick nodded and stood. He handed Jedrek his shirt and focused on his lion. He stared into Jedrek's eyes as he let the lion surge forward once more, and this time, it flowed out of him more slowly, sensually. Easier. He bumped Jedrek's belly with his head and Jedrek knelt down in front of him. He leaned forward and pressed their foreheads together for a moment before standing and pulling his shirt back on.

"Come on. I'll walk."

They'd gone further than Nick realized, and it took them several minutes to walk back to the road, and then another few to get to the end to Zaire's house. She was waiting for them on the porch, sitting at a small cafe table that hadn't been there before. Around her chair were a dozen stones, all sparkling in the morning sunlight.

"I sent the boys home," Zaire said. "Rowan is such an innocent. I think he's going to blush every time he sees you."

Nick growled and she laughed.

"I know. I sent a boy to do a woman's job. Should have known you two would have been at each other all night. The signs were all there. Jedrek, would you go inside and get our drinks? Oh, and grab the folder you carried in. I'm curious as to what is inside."

Jedrek sent another look Nick's way before heading inside to do as she'd asked. Nick prowled up the steps and sniffed Zaire's leg. She didn't smell right. Something was off. The fire she'd held before was still there, but it had soured somehow.

"Time to change back, Nick. We need to talk about a few things, and I need a human voice."

Nick huffed but changed again. "Ow."

His muscles protested the back-and-forth of his change, but he stood and stretched, allowing everything to pop back into place. Jedrek opened the door and tossed his pants out then carried out his folder and little tray of glasses.

"If I have to get naked to shift, it shouldn't be such a big deal for me to be naked."

"It's not," Zaire said. "I'm certainly enjoying the view."

Jedrek smirked and sat down at the table. Nick tugged on his pants and joined them.

"Since my son was born, I have been determined to protect him from the darkness in this world. My coven was— is— under constant threat. We no longer live together, as I created this place as a safe haven for my son and his coven. I'm afraid I need to go to them now, however. Keziah was right; I never should have touched that magic without their support. I did know better."

Nick scowled and looked out over the peaceful street. She'd created a haven for them, one he'd love to have been a part of, even if it was all cookie cutter and a little more Stepford than he'd like. "You kept what happened to me from happening to him."

"Yes. But then I learned that other children had been taken. When we found Ben and the others, something in me broke. And to learn they had a young magic user... I swore I would find them and stop them."

"We all did," Jedrek added.

"The time is now. We have the pieces we need."

"Whatever you need from me, I'm in," Nick said.

"I'll be with my coven for a few days. Jedrek, I leave my home under your protection until I return."

Nick had no doubt this woman would do anything to keep her son safe. He liked that about her.

"Nick, let your lion grow stronger while I'm gone. When we're back, we have work to do."

Nick grinned and the lion in him puffed up. They would get stronger, together. He glanced at Jedrek and his hellhound stared back. And he knew just the guy to help with the job.

JEDREK

Screaming children woke Jedrek the next morning from a dead sleep. Up and out the door in seconds, he hit the grass fully-shifted. It took him that long to realize that the screams weren't terror-filled ones, but more of laughter and playing. Nick roared beside him, obviously as worried as Jedrek over the sounds. There were a dozen adults in the road along with several children. All of them didn't quite seem to know what to do about the fully shifted lion and hellhound staring at them.

But Jedrek only had eyes for one of them. She was achingly familiar. *Sophie.*

"Nick, Jedrek, sorry we woke you," Keziah said.

"Jedrek," Izzy gasped.

She stared at him in his shifted form, and he moved closer. Slowly, so he didn't scare her any more than she already was. It took her a second, and then she smiled, about the time Sophie yelled "Simba!"

Nick was hit with a bundle of excited six-year-old a second later and, if Jedrek had been in his human form, he'd have died laughing.

Nick froze, clearly having no idea what to do. Of course, by that time, the other two kids, Leandra's two-year-old twins, had shifted into their lion form and were pouncing on Nick, too.

"Oh shit," Leandra gasped. She'd walked out of a house across the street a moment too late to stop the cub attack from happening.

Keziah didn't seem to know what to do either. Jedrek finally took pity on Nick and growled. The cubs froze then looked at him. It only took a second to decide he was something that needed to be explored. They tripped over their feet scrambling over to him, but Sophie stayed with Nick, petting him and cooing softly. Nick looked terrified.

Jedrek growled once more, a warning to the cubs to behave, before changing back into his human form. Sophie took one look at him and let out a squeal that nearly burst his ear drums. She let Nick go and ran to him, leaping into his arms the moment she was close enough. "Uncle Jed!"

"Hey, Peanut."

She tucked her face into his neck and wrapped her little arms around his neck. "I missed you."

"I missed you, too. Have you been having fun?"

She raised her head and beamed. "It's fun here! I get to grow plants with Rowan and Calder lets us lay in the stream with him and he shows us all the pretty rocks in the water. And Keziah made me a pretty bracelet, see? He said I can't take it off, though, because it's special just for me."

Jedrek recognized it as a protective charm and sent Keziah a look of thanks. "That all sounds fun."

"Uh-huh. And now Ariella and Lionel are here and they're baby lions and Zaire said I could play with them today if their mommy said it was okay and she did! And now *Simba* is here, Uncle Jed!"

Nick made a protesting sound so Jedrek carried Sophie over to him and knelt down. "This isn't Simba, Peanut. This is my friend, Nick. Can you say hi?"

She looked doubtful. "Nick isn't a lion name, Uncle Jed."

"Well, it's this lion's name."

She sighed, clearly disappointed. "Hi, Nick the lion."

Nick made a little grumbling sound and bumped his nose against her hand.

"He wants you to pet him," Jedrek whispered.

Nick glared at him but couldn't exactly deny it. Sophie reached out and touched his nose, then ran her hand down his face.

"Good girl. Now let me go say hi to your mom."

She gave Nick one last pat then looped her arm back around Jedrek's neck. Izzy had tears in her eyes as he approached and stepped into him when he held out his free arm. "Everyone okay?"

"Yep. Solomon and Cody finally got their heads out of their...uh, nether regions."

"Uncle Jed, what's a never region?"

"I'll tell you when you're bigger," Izzy said with a laugh. "And it's about time. Sorry we woke you and your..."

She looked at Nick expectantly then back at Jed.

"Mate," Jedrek said.

Nick made another of his chuffing noises, which seemed to be a call to the young lion cubs. One of them tried to jump on his back and the other was using his tail as a chew toy.

"Mate," Izzy repeated. "That's... new."

"Yep."

"Is that a... hellhound thing?"

Nick chuffed again and tried to walk away from the cubs, but they just followed him. He circled Jedrek and the others, but the cubs didn't leave him alone. He finally sent a pleading glance Jedrek's way. He whistled and both cubs paused and looked his way.

"I can get them. I'm sorry."

"They're fine, Leandra," Jedrek said softly. "Nick just isn't used to cubs. It's good for him to get to know them."

"Zaire said he's new and—"

"He won't hurt them. It's more that he's having trouble controlling his shift at this point. His instincts are at the forefront, but you know as well as I do that an alpha couldn't hurt cubs."

Leandra nodded, but she still kept her eyes on them. He couldn't blame her. Wild lions would very much hurt the cubs of another alpha male. Not Nick though. His instincts might still be messed up, but not to that level. No, Nick was more terrified of them. It made him laugh all the more.

Nick darted a few steps away, and the cubs stumbled after him. He let them get close, then darted away again. They made little chuffing sounds at him obviously enjoying their hunt, and he huffed right back before rushing forward another few steps.

"I wanna play tag with Nick the lion," Sophie said.

"After breakfast," Jedrek said. "Nick! Food!"

Nick turned, and the cubs both pounced on him, finally capturing their prey. If looks could kill, Jedrek would be a dead man. He cackled. "Come on. Hurry up. I'm hungry."

Nick hurried back to his side with both cubs chasing after him.

"Mom wanted you and Nick to talk to Leandra," Keziah said. "I thought we'd play with the cubs for a while, maybe wear them out and get them down for a morning nap. Rowan said he'd watch them with me."

"I can help," Izzy said.

Leandra chewed her bottom lip nervously. "They can come with me. I don't want to cause any trouble."

"No trouble at all," Izzy replied. "I'm hoping I can get you to return the favor for me sometime with Sophie."

Leandra smiled and gave her a nod. "I can do that."

"Good. Then the boys can go eat and we'll let the kids play for a while, and then we'll watch the twins while you talk to them. Sound like a plan?"

Leandra nodded.

"Works for us, too."

"But Uncle Jed, I want to stay with you."

"Not right now, Peanut. Let me go get breakfast, and then we'll come back out, okay?"

She pouted but nodded.

Nick bumped against him, so Jedrek grabbed his mane and held tight.

"So, um... everyone's okay?" Izzy asked again.

"Yep."

Jedrek waited her out. It was a little mean; he knew exactly who she wanted to ask about.

"Um. Walt and Shelly? Doing well?"

"They're great. Shelly's bossing us all around as usual and they keep getting closer. It's nice to see."

She smiled as Sophie skipped away with the cubs chasing after her now that Nick was being boring and not moving.

"Achim and Teague?"

"Doing well."

"Vice?"

"Same."

Nick huffed, and Jedrek smoothed his hand over his neck.

Izzy sucked in a breath and finally met his gaze. "And Calli?"

"She's good, Iz."

"I thought she'd come see me when... you know."

"She might. Zaire doesn't have an open door policy, and Meshaq promised he'd give you time."

"Yeah."

"If you want to see her, you should call her. Hell, text her, Iz."

Keziah glanced at them, before walking slowly away to give them a little privacy.

"O-okay."

"Now, we're going to go eat. I'll be around later."

Izzy nodded and followed Keziah. Nick sent a questioning huff Jedrek's way, but he simply gripped his mane again and made his way back to the house they were calling home for the next little while.

Nick stayed in his lion form when they got inside, finding a sunny spot in the dining room and stretching out. Jedrek tried not to laugh at him as he began snoring a few minutes later. Instead, he rummaged in the fridge. He'd learned enough from Walt to know how to make a few things, even though he tended to just eat what Walt gave him or eat take out. The problem was, there wasn't anything in the fridge. And the freezer had things that had instructions like defrost overnight and Jedrek was way too hungry to deal with that.

He went back onto the porch and waved Keziah over.

"Everything okay?"

"Just, you know, wondering if you had some bread and pb & j we could use?"

Keziah made a face and gave him a disappointed look. "You need to get me a grocery list."

"I know. I mean, we found some stuff last night that said soup so we just heated it up and it was fine, but I thought there'd be some eggs or something in the fridge, but all I have are some mostly stale donuts, and not gonna lie, the soup didn't really do it for me. Tasted good, but, you know—"

"You're a shifter. You eat a lot. Got it. I'll take care of getting the kitchen stocked for you. Mom normally handles that, but—"

"Yeah, we just need something to eat."

Keziah laughed. "I'll take care of it. I've got eggs and stuff at my house. I think someone made some fresh bread. I'll ask Rowan. He'll know."

"Thanks, Keziah."

"No problem. I'll be right back."

Jedrek went back into the dining room and found Nick still dozing in the patch of sunlight. He sank down onto the floor and leaned against him, resting his head and shoulders against Nick's side. Nick huffed and wiggled a little to get comfortable.

"There's no breakfast food," Jedrek said with a yawn. Nick was nice and warm.

Nick huffed.

"Keziah's getting us food."

Nick didn't seem to care either way.

"I think it's good Zaire wanted you to talk to Leandra. One, the lion thing. Two, she's the only mother we've found from the whole magical kids kidnapping thing."

Nick moved beneath him and Jedrek opened his eyes. Nick looked stunned. He growled again.

"Uh, did I not tell you that?"

Nick moved and with a grumble, Jedrek moved. Nick shifted back then knelt naked on the floor beside him. "You told me. I'm just thinking about it differently now. I had time to process, I guess. But why does Zaire want *me* to talk to her?"

Jedrek had a few theories. "Maybe she thinks you need a pride? And she happens to know a lioness with two cubs who could use an alpha?"

Nick made a noise that was deeply disturbing. "She's not matchmaking?"

Jedrek grinned and tugged Nick closer. Nick, being the ass he was, wiggled his way around until he was back in the sunny spot with Jedrek as his pillow. "No, not matchmaking romantically. But maybe pack-making would be a better word."

Nick scoffed. "You made that up."

"Yep."

"I can't be an alpha. I don't know what I'm doing."

"You *are* an alpha, and even if Zaire isn't trying to find you a pride, she's probably trying to get you to talk to another lion who knows more about this stuff than she does."

Nick huffed. "Why doesn't Leandra have a pride already? And if she does, why didn't she take her kids there for safety?"

"I don't know."

"I mean, she should have run home, right? I'd have gone to my brothers if some weird shit went down. If you hadn't been there, and things had gone differently when I found the house, I'd have... maybe, talked to my brothers. Especially if they'd told me they knew. Damn. This is confusing. My head is spinning."

Jedrek ran his fingers through Nick's messy hair. "So maybe talking to her is good."

"It'll just piss me off."

"How so?" Jedrek asked.

"Because if she went into hiding, that means her family, pride, whatever they're called, are a bunch of asshats. It'll piss me off."

Jedrek grinned. "You're so scary."

"Shut up. Rub my head."

Jedrek complied, giving Nick's hair a gentle tug before he ran his finger through it. "My ass is going to be numb in a minute. Why are we sitting on the floor?"

"Because that's where the sunny spot is."

Obviously.

Jedrek leaned against the wall and continued stroking Nick's hair, even as he began to breathe deeply and evenly, drifting to sleep once more. His legs went numb and his ass ached, but he didn't move. Damn, he had it bad.

He heard Keziah approaching and the gentle knock on the door. "Come in."

Nick stirred and bumped his head against Jedrek's hand. He started petting again.

Keziah carried a canvas bag into the kitchen, eyeing them curiously.

"Nick is apparently not a morning person."

Nick huffed. "I'm tired."

Jedrek grinned as Keziah began to unpack the bag. "I wore him out."

Keziah laughed. "Shifting is wearing him out, although I'm sure you're helping. He needs more calories than he's been getting, especially if he hasn't shifted before. Just... stay there. I brought random food. I'll cook, but just this once."

He glared at them both, but Nick didn't bother opening his eyes. "Thanks, Keziah," he rumbled. "Comfy."

"Nick doesn't know much about this place," Jedrek said. "And honestly neither do I."

"There wasn't a question there," Keziah said as he found measuring cups and a bowl in the cabinets.

Jedrek scowled at him, but Nick wiggled around so he was on his back and opened his eyes.

"I don't get why Zaire had to leave. I don't get any of this shit, honestly. But that's what I want to know first."

Keziah made a huffing sound that Jedrek recognized. Frustration. He'd heard it a lot the past couple of days spending time with Nick.

"Okay, the easy answer is, she went to be with her coven. But I know that doesn't tell you much, so I guess I'll tell you more. Which is weird, because Mom is big on secrets, and part of me feels like she did this on purpose so I'd have to step up. But that's part of the story. Nick, do you know anything about awen?"

"Nope."

"What about elemental magic?"

"Like fire, water, earth, air? That?"

"Exactly. Mostly it's referred to as elemental magic, but those of us with the gift are known as awen. It's more common than you think, but mostly, awen don't have enough power to do much, and then, we're only as powerful as our coven. Needless to say, there aren't that many really powerful covens around because it takes four powerful awen to make one."

"But you guys are," Nick said.

"Yes. Mom made sure of it. When I was little, she knew I'd be powerful like her. She has a decent coven, but they didn't really help her much. Honestly, she's a lot stronger than the rest of her coven."

Nick grumbled again and sat up. "So how do you get a coven?"

Keziah grinned and began mixing ingredients in the bowl with his hands. Whatever it was, it looked disgusting.

"Well, if you're anyone *but* my mom, you wait for fate to bring you together and birds sing and butterflies flutter about and you know in your heart that it's *right*."

Nick snorted. "And your mom?"

"She pretty much searched the continent until she found kids about my age who were also strong, and she also figured out a way to make this place. She brought all our families together so we grew up here, and she's brought in a few other people since then so we were *well-rounded*. Her words. Not mine."

Jedrek was fascinated. He'd never known all of this. "She's fierce."

"Yeah," Keziah said proudly. "She is."

"So which element are you?" Nick asked.

"You tell me."

Keziah began rolling the mixture into little balls and placing them on a baking sheet. Jedrek couldn't deny being curious, but Nick was still using him as a pillow so he didn't move. He really wanted to know what was in the bowl, though. He stroked Nick's hair and waited as his mate pondered Keziah's request. *His mate*. Jedrek liked the sound of it. He tightened his hold on Nick's hair, drawing his attention.

"What?"

"Nothing."

Nick grunted and turned his attention back to Keziah. "You're fire. Like Jedrek and the hellhounds. You smell like... fire. So does your mom."

"Yep."

"And that Rowan guy. He's earth. He smells like trees and the forest. And... am I earth too?"

"Yep."

"Yeah. Leandra smells like warm trees. That's weird. But that's what she smells like, and I figure I'm the same as her. The wolves smell like trees, too. But more... forest."

"Exactly. Most true shifters have earth powers."

"Most, but not all."

"Nope," Keziah said. "Not all. Because we like to keep things complicated."

"Hmm. So how does my brother fit into all this? I mean, you guys are with the fire goddess. And he has the sisters who I guess have... minions, too. What's the word?" Nick looked up at Jedrek.

"What do you mean?"

"Like minions of the goddess, who report to her or whatever. What do you call them?"

"Technically, we're her animal to call. Each goddess has specific creatures whose magic is associated with theirs. There isn't a word for us. Not that I know," Jedrek explained.

"Only the goddesses?"

"Yeah."

"But how come there are four types of magic and only three goddesses? Oh, does the mother goddess count as one? And how come my brother doesn't have, you know, minions?"

"We aren't minions," Jedrek complained.

"Power is passed from mother to daughters," Keziah said. He'd switched to cracking eggs in a bowl, but he looked deep in thought.

"But isn't your coven all guys?"

"Yes."

"This makes no sense."

"Awen can be men or women," Keziah said.

"Someone needs to make up their mind." Nick wiggled around, moving to the new spot where the sun was shining through the windows. When he finally settled, he looked up at Keziah once more. "Tell me more about this place."

"My mom won it in a poker game."

"No shit?"

"No shit. A lot of awen use their gifts for good, and we sell stuff. But it doesn't exactly make us millionaires. Mom has a wicked good poker face, though, and ended up with cash and this land. I guess someone in her coven had a vision about it or something. She's a little vague on those details."

That news didn't surprise Jedrek at all. Zaire was often vague on details.

"But she got it before I was born and built us a house here. Then she started doing other stuff. She wants us to be self-sufficient as much as we can, because letting people through the wards isn't awesome. Of course, after Henry and Sam were attacked, she had us working like crazy to figure out a new way to make wards. Now, no one can enter the wards who mean us harm as long as my coven is together within them."

"Huh. That's good."

Jedrek hadn't known that. He wondered if Meshaq did.

"Yeah. She wanted us to figure out a way to make the wards at the clinic stronger, and we did, but not as strong as ours. No way was she making my coven stay there with as many sick shifters as are coming in and out all the time. She thought about having Vaughn and Sam come here with the kids so we'd have more kids to grow up with, but she told me later that she knew there was no way Vaughn would give up his practice and leave his pack behind, so she didn't ask. And the kids needed their dads, so even though they had a little more risk, she let it go."

"What happened to Henry and Sam? What attack?"

"Mrs. Foote kidnapped them," Jedrek said. "Created a portal in the living room of their house and took them."

"Bitch. We really need to find her."

"Yeah," Jedrek said. "We really do."

"Breakfast is almost ready. You want to get dressed?"

Jedrek glanced down and realized belatedly that Nick was laying on the floor completely naked. He chuckled and Nick glared up at him. "If I could shift like you, this wouldn't be an issue. It's not fair."

"That's because hellhounds aren't shifters like you," Keziah said. "They get their power directly from the goddess. They shift...I guess you'd say they shift magically and not physically. The same result, but a different process."

Nick growled as he rolled to the side and stood. "Then pants should be optional."

"I'm not complaining," Jedrek said. He tried not to leer but was pretty sure he failed.

"I'm not either," Keziah said.

Jedrek smirked when Nick smacked his own forehead and left the room. Jedrek watched him go, enjoying the view the entire way.

NICK

After breakfast, Nick worked on a grocery list while Jedrek showered. He'd started to go in with him, but then he'd be all sex-stupid again and he really wanted to talk to Leandra. The questions from Keziah had helped him fill in a few blank spots, but he couldn't help wondering what prompted Zaire to make sure he spent time with the other lion shifter. She had a plan. If he'd learned nothing else in the Q&A with Keziah, it was that his mother *always* had a plan. He checked the recipe for the sausage ball things Keziah had made them for breakfast and added the ingredients. Between him and Jedrek, they'd eaten the whole batch. They should learn how to make them. Possibly in bulk.

He'd tried suggesting that Keziah just get them a bunch of microwave dinners, but Keziah had paled before informing him that there wasn't a microwave in the kitchen. Apparently, microwaves were bad. Or something. Nick wasn't sure. Maybe they just disapproved of his general laziness when it came to cooking? It didn't matter. From the sounds of things, Keziah was going to make sure they had food and that was all that mattered. Although... would it be rude to put more lube on the list? They were going through the bottle Jedrek brought pretty fast.

Jedrek came back into the room, dressed and with his hair slicked back. He'd trimmed the sides and Nick liked it. He abandoned the list and grabbed Jedrek instead.

"Can't get enough of you," he murmured before he nipped at the edge of Jedrek's lips.

"Same," Jedrek replied. He pulled away though, and Nick growled in protest. "We promised Keziah we'd talk to Leandra. She's anxious and he's worried."

Something in Nick flipped at the words and he managed to pull back. "Fine. But we're continuing this later."

He grabbed Jedrek's hand and dragged him outside. The kids were still playing, but they ran for them when they caught sight of him. The cubs were still in their shifted form, and they bounded up to Nick and batted his legs.

"They want up," Sophie said as she held up her arms to Jedrek.

Nick stared at them.

Jedrek picked Sophie up and gave Nick an expectant look. He sighed but leaned down and managed to wrangle the twins into his arms.

"Who are you?" Sophie asked.

"That's Nick the lion," Jedrek said.

"Oh. Nick can change into a lion like Ariella and Lionel can?"

Jedrek nodded. The little girl stared at him again.

"I wanna be a lion, too."

"No can do, Soph. You're supposed to be a little girl."

Her lower lip began to wobble and Nick looked on in panic. He couldn't handle crying kids. He could barely manage the two wriggling in his arms and trying to climb onto his head. He heard a growl and the cubs froze. He looked toward the sound and found Leandra staring at her kids. They settled after the noise, draping themselves over him like he was their own personal climbing tree.

Keziah and Rowan came out of one of the houses down the street and began walking their way. "Who wants to go check on the straw-berries with me?"

Three little heads perked up.

"We can pick some and make something in the kitchen," Rowan said.

Before Nick could even process the words, the cubs had leapt from his arms and were high tailing it over to them. Sophie wiggled her way down from Jedrek and ran over, too.

"Smooth," Jedrek muttered.

"This whole communal living thing is weird."

"Bad weird?"

Nick took a second to think about it. He wasn't used to being around so many people, that was for sure. He'd spent a lot of time alone over the past few years. "No. Not bad."

"Just different."

"Yeah. I mean, I'm pretty much a loner, so being around so many people is... well, not what I'm used to."

"I get it. We should probably do a patrol, make sure the wards are stable."

"I take it that's a hint to get moving."

Jedrek lifted his brows and Nick sighed. All he wanted to do was go find a sunny spot, convince Jedrek to shift with him, and maybe curl up together and take a nap. Was that too much to ask?

"Leandra, let's walk," Jedrek said.

Nick grumbled again. They started walking toward the gate and she settled into step beside them. They hadn't made it half way down the street when she spoke.

"I don't want an alpha."

Nick huffed. "Good. Cause I don't want a pack. Pride. Whatever."

She scowled. "You don't?"

"God, no. Why would I?"

Jedrek sighed. "Is this really the conversation you want to have?"

Nick turned to glare at him. Then noticed that Leandra had done the same thing. Jedrek held up his hands in surrender and stepped back. "Fine, do this your way."

He started walking again, and Nick followed.

Leandra moved back beside him again. "*Every* alpha wants a pack."

"Not this one."

"You *should* want a pack."

"I don't."

Leandra sighed.

Jedrek did, too.

"What? The only thing I want is a sunny spot and my... Jedrek. And lube. Jed, can we add lube to the grocery list or is that weird?"

Jedrek coughed. "Well, it's weird now."

Nick glanced at Leandra who was looking at him like he was from another planet. "What? Lube. It's a requirement for the kind of sex we're having. And I want a lot more of it. Hence, more lube."

Leandra stared at him like he was a lunatic for a minute longer, then she burst out laughing. Jedrek wrapped his arms around Nick from behind and lowered his head into Nick's hair. It only took him a second to realize Jedrek was laughing at him, too.

"You're both assholes."

Leandra laughed harder. "And assholes need lube."

Jedrek made a weird choking sound, so Nick elbowed him in the stomach. "A man has needs."

It took them a second to stop laughing, but when they did, Leandra gave him a look and started walking again. He grabbed Jedrek's hand and stayed with her.

"You don't... want to have sex with me, do you?"

Nick flinched. He couldn't help it. What was he supposed to say to that? "Uh, no? I mean, it's not you. It's me. I, you know—" Nick pointed awkwardly at Jedrek. "And you're pretty and all, but—" He again gestured to Jedrek.

"So you're gay?"

Nick floundered again. "Well... I mean... technically no? I mean, bi for sure. But Sawyer says I'm pan. There was this whole thing about Captain Jack and aliens, and honestly, I'm not sure I understand."

Leandra didn't look comforted by the news. "So you might want to have sex with me one day."

"I mean..." Nick looked to Jedrek for help. "I don't know what I'm supposed to say here."

"The truth," Jedrek said softly. He flared his eyes at Nick, but it wasn't in anger. It gave him confidence to say what he wanted. That he wouldn't screw up if he spoke the truth.

Nick's eyes flared in return, and he turned back to Leandra. Everything was sharper through the lion's view. Leandra stepped back.

"Look, I don't know what all this mate stuff means, okay? But apparently Jedrek is mine. It's new. And I don't know shit about shit right now. So will I want to have sex with you some day in the future? Maybe. How the fuck should I know? I don't know what I'm having for lunch today. But for now, big guy here is all I want to have sex with and, no offense but Jedrek said to be honest, the thought of having sex with you kinda makes me feel sick. So there's that. But, um, no offense."

Jedrek coughed out another laugh and Leandra stopped walking again.

Nick sighed and turned to her. "I'm terrible at this."

"No. You're actually not," Leandra said. "Zaire said you didn't know anything about lions or prides or packs or anything."

"I didn't even know most of this shit was real until yesterday. I was raised with a bunch of other kids who didn't know anything and... yeah. It's not like I had some lion dad to show me the ropes or whatever. Papa Smith was what I had, and he was human. I think." Nick turned to Jedrek. "Please tell me my parents were human."

Jedrek raised a brow. "Sorry to break it to you, but I doubt it."

"Shit. Does Sawyer know?"

"Probably not. You should ask him."

"Dammit. How'd she end up with three of us if she wasn't something different? You're probably right. Papa just put up with us all, though. He was cool like that. A go with the flow guy. Could fix anything you put in front of him, though, as long as it didn't involve food in the kitchen. Mama Thea said my loathing of all things cooking-related was from him." A pang of sadness went through him once more at their memory. Their loss was fresh in his mind, a wound that never fully healed. Even though he had his brothers, Nick still picked up the phone to call Mama Thea sometimes before he remembered she wouldn't be there to answer.

Jedrek tugged him close and he breathed in his warm scent. A feeling of calm flooded through him, and he breathed again, chasing the elusive, amazing scent that was Jedrek. "Damn, you smell good."

"We'll call your brothers later," Jedrek said. "Check on them."

"They said they'd call if there was any change."

"I know. Let's call anyway."

"Yeah. I don't want to nag."

"They need you to nag. Be a big brother."

"You have brothers?" Leandra asked.

"Yeah. They're both kinda hurt right now, but they said I should come and get this magic shit figured out. It's important. I've been trying to find the people who held me captive as a kid since... well, since I was a kid and escaped."

Leandra made another noise. "You were... one of them."

"Yeah."

"That's what would have happened to my cubs if I hadn't escaped. They would have..." Her voice broke and Nick stepped closer.

"But that didn't happen. You got them out. And now Zaire thinks you can help us find them."

"I will. As long as..."

"If it puts your kids at risk, then we don't do it. Period. They aren't getting their hands on any other cubs. Not on my watch."

They walked again, reaching the gate and turning to walk along it. Jedrek's eyes stayed flamey, and he seemed to be inspecting the wards.

"Can you see the wards?"

"Yes," Jedrek said.

"Can I?"

"Probably not. You should try."

Nick focused and let the lion take charge again. He didn't shift, though, even though he'd kind of offered to let the lion out. "Huh, that's weird."

"What?"

"I think I'm communicating with the lion side or something."

"That's what happens. He's part of you, not separate."

"It should be seamless," Leandra added. "You should not be able to distinguish between the two sides so easily."

"I guess I'm learning."

"I cannot see wards," Leandra said. "I can feel them."

"Yeah. I feel 'em. But... no, I can't see anything but fence." He turned back to Jedrek. "I kinda want to run."

"So let's run. Leandra?"

She glanced between them for a second before making her decision. She nodded. Nick grabbed the hem of his shirt but then paused. "Oh, uh, yeah. This whole getting naked thing is weird."

"Tell me about it."

Jedrek snorted and shifted.

"Asshole."

Leandra snickered. "I don't really care, though. But yeah, it's awkward. I grew up shifting, but only around my... family."

Nick got it. It was one thing for his brothers to see him naked, but some stranger... yeah, not so much. "I'll turn my back and you turn yours."

"Deal."

Jedrek made another noise, this one more of a hurry up huff, and Nick grabbed his neck in reply. "So not fair." He got a head butt to the gut in reply. "Fine, I'm hurrying."

Nick stripped quickly before letting the lion out to play. Dr. Vaughn hadn't been lying when he said he'd be sore, but it got easier every time. It was nice. He breathed deeply and caught the scent of Leandra's lion. He turned. She stood back, muscles tense. She was ready to run.

He huffed at her. Like he was suddenly going to hump her in this form. He wasn't that out of his mind. He turned back to Jedrek, licked the side of his face, and took off running. He heard the growl of annoyance behind him, but couldn't exactly laugh in this form. He was fast, though, but not as fast as either Jedrek or Leandra. Within seconds, they'd both caught up to him. There was a path around the edge of the property, about twenty feet from the fence itself to the tree line. It was smart. They couldn't use the trees to climb and miss the fence altogether. Although Nick was pretty sure the wards didn't work that way. He wondered how far up in the air it went. Was there like a no-fly zone over the entire place as well? It didn't seem like it kept actual birds out. He saw enough of them flying around. Squirrels too. One ran along the edge of the fence as they approached before leaping to safety on the other side of the fence.

Nick breathed it all in, letting the lion teach him. Scents, sights, sounds. He processed it all in ways he'd never known, not even as a child. He'd never been allowed this freedom to run. And with a pack. The word tripped his human mind, but the lion knew. It wasn't a possibility. It was. They were his pack. They circled the property, so fast together. Nick skidded to a stop and roared. The sound echoed and everything stilled. Jedrek and Leandra both leaned against him, running up and down his sides. Scenting him. It was right. True. Complete.

Nick roared again, unable to stop the lion from exclaiming his power. Leandra's voice joined his, then Jedrek's. He looked at them both, and something in Leandra's face informed him. He just knew. His instincts led him, and he turned back toward the houses. She followed, sticking close to his side. And Jedrek, his beautiful scary hellhound, walked beside him, too. He didn't have to go far. The cubs were running toward them, being chased by Keziah, Izzy, Rowan, and Sophie. They were being told to stop, but they wouldn't. Of course they wouldn't. Their alpha had called them.

Lionel reached him first, skidding into his legs as he stopped. He made a chuffing roar, which wasn't much more than a squeak, and Nick leaned down and licked him on the head. It was a good try for a little guy. Lionel rolled onto his back, and Nick gave him a good sniff. Ariella whined, wanting his attention, too. Nick bumped her with his nose, and she tried to show off her roar as well. Hers was a bit chirpy, but Nick gave her a lick of approval. She rolled onto her back and he scented her. The humans, next. He prowled forward, reaching Sophie first. Izzy held onto her daughter's shoulders, clearly not understanding what was happening. Nick smelled them, but no. They weren't his. They belonged to another.

Keziah and Rowan stood together, both looking nervous but excited. He smelled them and... paused. Maybe. Not yet. But maybe. He turned back to the rest, approaching Jedrek first. He nuzzled his mate's neck and felt his warm breath along his neck. Mmm. Warm. The sun was out, warming the pavement of the long road into the neighborhood. He'd just stretch out and—

Jedrek growled.

Nick huffed. Fine. The lion was satisfied anyway, so Nick let him drift back and shifted back into his human form. The cubs immediately pounced. Leandra chuffed at him, then darted back toward the gate. Jedrek gave him a look and started for their house.

"What?" Nick griped. "I didn't do anything."

Keziah snickered, drawing Nick's attention. "You were totally going to take a nap, weren't you?"

"Yeah, well. What's wrong with naps? Nothing. Not one single thing is wrong with naps."

Rowan hid his smile behind his hand.

"Yeah, well, you're all—" Nick glanced down at the kids staring up at him with big eyes, "—stinky."

"That's not nice, Nick the lion. You shouldn't say someone is stinky. Mommy says so."

Izzy wasn't hiding her smile at all. "Exactly, Nick the lion. Be nice."

Nick huffed and walked away. "I'll show you nice," he grumbled.

Leandra reappeared beside him, fully dressed with his clothes in her hand. "Thought you might want these."

"Yeah, well, I'm naked. Everybody can just deal with it."

"But Nick the lion, you're supposed to wear pants. Mommy says so."

Nick growled and grabbed the clothes from Leandra's hand. He pulled them on and glared. "There. Everyone happy now?"

"Mommy, I think he needs a nap. He's cranky. When I'm cranky, you say I need a nap."

Nick threw his hands in the air and followed after Jedrek. He found him sitting on the porch. Laughing his ass off.

Nick plopped down in front of him and leaned back into the vee of Jedrek's legs. He huffed again, and Jedrek wrapped his arms around him.

"Poor baby," Jedrek rumbled against his ear. "Did everyone gang up on you?"

They had but... Nick didn't exactly mind. Leandra sat next to him on the step and leaned into Jedrek. The twins climbed on her and settled on her lap. Izzy and Sophie sat down beside them. Keziah and Rowan sat in the grass, close enough to reach if Nick wanted.

"Pride," Leandra murmured. "I... wasn't expecting that to happen."

Nick shrugged. He wasn't either. He didn't really want to confess that, though. He had a question or two to ask. Now wasn't the time. He'd just close his eyes for a minute and ask Jedrek next time they had a little privacy. Yeah. That's what he'd do.

JEDREK

In the week it took for Zaire to return, Nick settled into his lion skin and into their mating. They fucked multiple times a day, and Jedrek constantly wanted more. Leandra grew more and more comfortable around Nick, and after the first couple days of runs together, she began to seek out their company outside of their morning run. As much as she'd protested wanting an alpha, she seemed to want to be around Nick.

Jedrek couldn't blame her. There was a cool confidence to him that drew all of them closer to him. Keziah and Rowan came by every day. They showed both of them around, taught Nick about the different experiments they were doing, and basically just showed off a bit. They might as well have been cubs. The other two coven members, Calder and Emmett, were a little slower to warm up to them, but even they'd started to succumb to Nick's charm. Calder had shown up with a casserole the day before, and when Nick ate half of it before he could even say thanks, he'd won the awen's favor. Emmett just seemed to not like strangers, but then again, he also seemed slightly unwell. None of them talked about it, though, so Jedrek kept his observations to himself.

As to Sophie and the lion cubs, well, Nick was their favorite, no two ways about it. They'd finished lunch a half hour before, and Nick had immediately shifted. He'd gone onto the porch and stretched out in a sunny spot. Ariella and Lionel had shifted moments later, and after Jedrek untangled them from their clothes, they went and curled up by Nick's stomach. Sophie, not to be left out, decided to use Nick as her body pillow. She laid down on top of him, stuck her thumb in her mouth, and went to sleep.

Jedrek sat on the porch steps and leaned back against the railing. The other people who lived there, most of whom had kept their distance although Keziah insisted they were fine with them being there, walked past their house and raised hands in greetings. Newcomers were rare enough inside the wards, but the fact that they had a hellhound and a slightly out of control alpha lion on their hands had made them all cautious.

The kids had helped calm their fears, though, and the fact that Nick was good with them. Well, he put up with them. They followed him around and he acted like the big brother he was. Annoyed by their presence, but no one better mess with them. Ariella had fallen down the day before and skinned her knee. Nick had roared at the pavement for daring to hurt her. Needless to say, he was the little girl's hero.

It was almost like Nick was taking a vacation, letting himself be free from all the burdens of nine-to-five, or in his case, all the anger and fear of the past few years. Something in him had settled once they set the lion inside free, and Jedrek hoped it stuck. He really didn't want to go back to the way things were before. He really didn't want to lose Nick.

But they only had a few days before his vacation from work was over. He'd called in that first day and taken all the time off he had available. It wasn't much. Of course, they'd not counted on Zaire being gone so long with no word. Keziah told them not to worry, but Jedrek couldn't help wondering what was going on in the outside world. He'd spoken to Solomon a couple times, and all was well with his pack. Everything had gone quiet again, and Jedrek had a sneaking suspicion they were in the eye of the storm.

He couldn't have been more surprised when he saw movement down the street and looked up to see Zaire closing the front door of her house. He hadn't even known she was back. She caught sight of him and became a woman with a mission as she marched down the street to him. Before she could speak, though, he put a finger to his lips. She scowled, but kept quiet as she moved closer. He pointed and she looked at Nick and the cubs sleeping. Her eyes widened and she looked back at him. He grinned. He couldn't help it. He was as surprised as anyone at Nick's easy acceptance of the kids.

She leaned her head back toward her place and he nodded. He waited for her to get a few steps down the sidewalk before he spoke.

"Nick."

He kept his voice quiet and pitched low, but Nick heard. He opened one eye and glared sleepily at him. "Zaire is back. She wants to talk to us."

Nick made a questioning huff.

"No, stay with the cubs. I'll text Izzy and have her come stay with them. Wait until she gets here and come down. I don't want to wake them up, especially the twin terrors."

Nick huffed again and closed his eyes. Jedrek gave him one last look before following Zaire. He shot Izzy a text while they walked, and then he sat down with Zaire on her front porch.

"You look better," Jedrek said after a long quiet minute.

"So do you."

Jedrek shot her a look. "So?"

She looked ticked, but not necessarily at him. She stared down the road, watching as Izzy crossed to the house he and Nick were slowly starting to call home. "My coven is not strong enough to deal with the level of magic we found."

"Shit."

"I used more colorful language, but yes."

"So, do we have a plan B?"

Zaire continued to glare, this time turning her attention to Nick as he sauntered up the street in his lion form. He'd forgotten pants again. Jedrek was going to have to start carrying a pair around with him at all times.

She waited until Nick was close enough to hear her before she spoke. "I'm going to do something I swore I never would."

"Zaire—" He wanted to warn her away from what he was afraid she was about to do. Some doors, once opened, couldn't be closed again.

Nick growled, sensing the tension in the air as he climbed up the step and leaned into Jedrek's side.

"No, Jedrek. I am not going to command. I'm going to ask." She stared at Nick, taking another breath before she spoke again. "I'm going to ask my son's coven to attempt to break this magic apart."

Nick roared, and began shifting back. Jedrek groaned as the cubs began to chuff and howl, their little voices scared.

"Dammit, Nick."

"Sorry," Nick said once he'd shifted. "But Zaire, you can't do that. You said it wasn't safe. It hurt you."

"Because, as my son so wisely pointed out, I was an idiot and tried without the support of my coven. I did know better. Keziah, though. He's strong. And his coven is strong. If anyone can break this down, they can."

Nick paused as Izzy walked closer with upset kids in her arms. She tossed Nick a pair of sweatpants with a glare and he pulled them on. "Deal with this. You did it."

Nick sat down on the steps and let the cubs crawl onto his lap. They'd changed back into their human form and Izzy had put pull-ups on both of them but nothing else. Sophie held her mother's hand looking sleepy and confused. "What happened? Why'd you roar so loud?"

"Sorry guys. I just got a little grumpy. It happens sometimes."

"So you roared? That's not very nice, Nick. You scared us."

Trust a kid to point out the obvious.

Nick gave her a sheepish smile. "Sorry, Soph. Forgive me?"

She eyed him and considered her options. "Extra strawberries for dessert. And a popsicle for snack."

"You're a tough negotiator."

"Snack!"

Of course, Lionel only heard one word.

"Come on, kiddos," Izzy said. "Let's go get a snack. And then Nick gets to chase you down and put up with your cranky selves since you didn't get your nap. Won't that be fun?"

"Snack!"

Izzy beamed at them, and it was totally evil. Nick groaned as he watched her go.

Zaire, on the other hand, looked like she'd finally started putting the pieces together. Jedrek wondered what she'd say when she saw the others interacting with him. And she wouldn't have to wait long. Keziah, Rowan, and Leandra came out of the trees, each carrying a basket of vegetables. She'd never learned how to grow anything, so Rowan was teaching her about his kitchen and herb garden. Even Jedrek had been amazed at what he managed to grow in a field tucked away behind the trees.

Keziah glanced their way then began to hurry when he realized his mom was back. He stumbled up onto the porch and pushed his basket into Jedrek's arms. "Mom!"

"Hey, baby boy."

Keziah pulled her up and tugged her into a hug. "I was worried."

"I know. I'm sorry."

"You're better. I mean, I know you are because I can feel you are, but you are."

"I am."

"So?"

"No luck, honey."

Keziah looked grim, but determined. "Mom, you have to let us try."

"Kez—"

"No, Mom. Don't argue. We've been working for this day my entire life. We're done being sheltered. We're ready to be the coven you helped us become. We all agreed. When we helped the hell-hounds, we finally got a taste of how bad the magic had become. We're too sheltered here, but we can do good magic. If we can find who's doing this, it'll be *good*. Let us try."

She grabbed his arms and squeezed. "Okay."

"Mom, I mean it, we are read— wait, what?"

"You're right. You are ready. I want you to try."

"Who are you and what have you done with my mother?"

Zaire laughed and swatted him upside the head.

"Oh wait, there you are," Keziah said with a grin. "But seriously? You're going to let us try?"

"I am. This is too important and... it needs a full coven. I tried it my way and failed. It's time for you to step up."

Keziah grinned. "I've gotta go get the others."

"*Ask* them, Keziah. After dinner tonight, at dusk, we'll gather at the circle and discuss our options. *Talk* to them."

Keziah grinned and kissed her forehead. "Thanks, Mom."

He took off at a run, leaving them standing on the porch staring after him.

"What just happened?" Leandra asked.

Zaire breathed deeply and looked at her. "My son just grew up."

They all watched him running down the street. He seemed more like an excited teenager than a guy in his early twenties. He actually reminded Jedrek a little of Henry. Not in looks, but more in spirit.

"You're doing the right thing," Nick said quietly. "He's ready. You did what you could. You put yourself at risk first. But he's ready, Zaire."

Zaire turned to Nick and gave him an assessing look. "Is there something you want to tell me?"

Jedrek tensed at the dark tone in her voice.

"No. Is there something you want to ask me?"

Nick met her look with one of his own. Tension ratcheted up a notch. Leandra started to move, but Nick's hand on her arm stilled her.

"Did you make my son part of your pack?" Zaire asked.

"No. But if I had, it wouldn't concern you. He's an adult. That discussion would be between us."

She hissed.

Jedrek wanted to intervene. The instinct was there, nipping him forward, but he held himself back. Nick didn't need to be defended. It didn't change the fact that Jedrek wanted to, though.

"You've grown cocky."

"Eh, I was always cocky, Zaire. You met me at a not so great moment. But that's not really what you're pissed about."

She looked away, back in the direction her son had run. "He doesn't belong in a pack."

Nick shrugged. "Maybe he does. Maybe not. That's up to him to decide. I think it's more a case of whether or not the entire coven would be pack. It's all or nothing."

Zaire turned back to him. "Explain."

"The lion doesn't want only Keziah. I don't know. I just... my instincts say to wait for the other two. Keziah's good. So is Rowan. The other two aren't so definite, though, so we wait."

"Can a coven be pride?" Leandra asked. "I've not heard of that before."

Nick shrugged. "I only know what I feel."

"And your lion accepted Leandra and her cubs?"

"Yeah. I figured that's what you wanted anyway, right?"

Zaire smiled. "No, actually. I thought you'd want to talk to her about what happened to her, and perhaps learn a little more about being a lion."

"Oh. Well, I mean, I didn't think it was right to poke her about that stuff. Not when I don't know anything about that shit. It's magic stuff. That's your arena."

"But you are her alpha now."

Nick grumbled. "Look. I like her. You. Sorry, Leandra."

She chuckled. "It's fine. I like you, too."

"But your life is yours, you know? I'm not your boss or shit like that. I just...I'm here if you need me. That's all."

"I know."

"That's very sweet," Zaire said. "But before we attempt to work on the magic from the past, I think we need information about what they are up to now."

"Well, it's been like three years, right? The kids are two and add nine months or whatever. But closer than before, so I get your point."

"Leandra?"

Leandra moved beside Nick and grabbed his hand. Jedrek stood also and leaned into her other side. She grabbed onto the back of his shirt and held on. "You can ask me what you want."

Zaire's eyes softened, and she spoke in a calm, gentle tone. "Tell us what happened."

Leandra sucked in a breath. She turned to Nick. "There aren't a lot of lions anymore. I don't know if you know that, but, I mean, there's a lot of mating issues going on. Not a lot of cubs are born. I mean, some, yeah, but not like before. So my mom, she really wanted to find me someone to mate with who was... I don't know. Better."

"What's better?"

"Rich," Leandra said. "She was tired of being poor and thought if we could find some rich alpha lion or something that we'd have it made. But I just wanted to see the world, you know? Party a little, meet new people. See what was out there before I settled down so some guy could spend the next twenty years trying his best to knock me up."

"Ugh."

No one could say his mate wasn't eloquent. It was what Leandra needed to hear, though, because her hold on Jedrek eased a bit as she continued.

"So I decided to take a year to myself. I packed up and got on a bus and just rode. All the way to the east coast. I figured that was far enough, you know? I mean, I want to see the whole world, but at least

I could see places I'd never been. I left mom a note, which was shitty, but there was no way she was going to let me go."

"Did you let her know after?"

"Yeah. I called. She was pissed, but she got it. So I got a job as a waitress and just...lived. I was close to a college so there were always kids around partying and having fun. It was nice. No pressure. No rules. No alpha."

"Then what happened?" Nick asked.

"My year was almost up. I wasn't ready to go back. My friends were trying to convince me to apply to the college and I wanted to. So bad. I had the grades, but we didn't really have the money and I didn't want to take on a ton of debt. I don't know. But I was tempted. Then we went out to this bar, and there were shifters there. I hadn't really seen anyone in all that time. Which was weird, when I thought about it, but I mean, most shifters don't hang around community colleges so it wasn't all that crazy. But these guys, something was off about them."

"Off how?"

Leandra paused, trying to find words, then turned to Zaire. "You know how sometimes, when a shifter gets sick or something, they sort of... I don't know... fluctuate? Like sometimes they're strong and sometimes they aren't."

"Yes," Zaire said.

"It was like that but more. I mean, I thought one of the guys was human at first. But then he was a shifter again. It made no sense."

Jedrek and Zaire turned to each other. They'd seen that before as well, once before.

"Then what happened?" Nick asked.

"I guess they drugged me. I don't know. I know I sort of remember flashes. Some of it is crazy. Like, I swear there was this glowing white tiger. Other weird stuff, too. Lots of birds. They were so loud. And then, one day, my lion sort of woke up. I remember being so angry. Furious. Ready to hunt. One of the guys came in and

I just lost it. I shifted, but I guess they thought I couldn't. I... I killed him."

Nick grabbed her and pulled her close. Jedrek leaned in behind her and met his mate's angry gaze. Nick really wanted to find the bastards now, even more than before.

"Finish," Nick demanded.

"I killed him and got out. I ran for... I don't know. I stuck to the woods. Hunted. Made sure no humans saw me. When I finally came out of it, I realized it had been months since I was taken. And then I figured out that I was pregnant."

Zaire's breath caught, but Jedrek and Nick didn't budge.

"I hid. Stole what I needed and just stayed out of sight until the kids were born. I did what I had to do."

"Yes, you did. Why didn't you go home?" Nick asked.

"My mom would have gone nuts," Leandra said. "She'd have wanted to use the kids as a bargaining tool. I didn't want that. So I stayed away. But then... something changed and I was scared all the time. Convinced something was after me. I couldn't stop looking over my shoulder. So I ran some more. And then I found the bar and all the others gathered. I could tell they were as scared as I was. I listened. I heard them talking about Meshaq and Solomon. About how they were the champions. I thought if anyone would keep me safe, it would be them."

"You're safe now," Nick grumbled.

"Yeah, you are," Jedrek added.

"I don't know what happened to me," Leandra confessed. "But I know my kids aren't safe."

"They're safe here," Zaire said.

"How can you be sure? I don't know what they did. And everyone keeps saying that magic is messed up and doing weird things. What if they find me? What if they find my cubs?"

Zaire stood and held out her hand. "May I?"

Leandra tensed, but Nick made one of his many noises and she relaxed a bit before releasing her hold on Nick's hand and placing it in Zaire's. Zaire closed her eyes and Jedrek felt her magic rise. Heat and smoke and power. Nick began a rumbling growl, but Jedrek wrapped an arm around both Leandra and Nick. Nick looked at him, his eyes glowing the golden yellow of his lion. He flared his own. *Calm. It's okay. She's safe.*

Nick relaxed but the rumbling continued. It took a minute, and Zaire finally let out a breath. "You're safe here. Go love on those sweet babies of yours. You'll feel better."

Leandra let go of her hand and turned to Nick.

"Go. And don't let them eat all the Cheerios. The monsters."

With a laugh, she went down the porch and toward Izzy's house. Nick waited until she was inside before he leaned into Jedrek and breathed deeply. "I want to gut them."

"I know. Me, too." He turned to Zaire. "What aren't you telling us?"

Nick started, lifting his head and glaring. "What? Are they in danger? Are—?"

"No. They're safe here. The same dark magic was used against her. I can feel it. The remnants linger. We can use it."

Nick growled. "No."

Zaire scowled at him. "We need to—"

"No. She stays out of it. Use me."

"But—"

"Non-negotiable," Nick snapped. "They've still got their claws in me, and you're not touching her."

"Nick, you said it yourself. It's newer with her. Fresher. We have a better chance..."

"No."

Jedrek wanted to argue with him, but he couldn't. No way would he put Leandra at risk. But doing so meant Zaire would be digging into the deep wounds of Nick's past. They had no way of knowing what damage that magic had already done, or what would happen when it was torn open again.

NICK

He'd upset his mate.

Nick could think of nothing else.

They walked back to the house in silence. Nick could smell the fire burning in Jedrek. Anger. Bitter and sour.

"Jed, I—"

"I'm going to go check the wards."

"I can—"

"No." Jedrek turned to him and grabbed his neck. He pulled Nick close, resting their foreheads together. "I just need a few. I'll be back soon."

Before Nick could protest, Jedrek shifted and ran. Nick stared after him until he disappeared into the trees. He'd had no choice. Jedrek had to understand that. He couldn't let Zaire mess around with Leandra, not after everything she'd been through. And she had the kids to think about. No, it had to be him.

Nick went into the house and grabbed his phone. He ignored the messy sheets and abandoned, mostly-empty bottle of lube on the floor. Instead, he called the one other person he needed to talk to before the night's events took place.

"Nick?" Sawyer sounded stressed but happy to hear from him.

"Checking on you guys."

Sawyer sighed. "No change. Vaughn kicked us out. We're back at my house."

Nick didn't care for his defeated tone at all. "What's going on?"

"Absolutely *nothing*."

"Mikey?"

"Vaughn says he's hanging in. No change, but he's not getting worse. That's a good sign."

Nick paused, breathed for a moment. Jedrek's scent was strongest in the bedroom. It relaxed him, even if his mate couldn't be with him at the moment. "I want to talk to you about something."

"'K."

"We're trying something tonight. At dusk or whatever. I guess the time is important. I don't know anything about this shit." Nick paced. Walked the short walk down the hall to the kitchen, through the living room. And back again.

"Define something," Sawyer said.

"We're gonna do a spell. Keziah's coven, I mean. They're going to see if they can trace the magic in me so we can find Foote."

Nick could feel the stillness from the other end of the phone. He was pretty sure Sawyer had stopped breathing. He waited him out, let that big brain in his little brother's head process his words for a few seconds.

"*Nick.*"

"I know the timing is fucked up. But is there ever gonna be a good time for this? No. Time is now, when as you said, absolutely nothing is going on. Right?"

Sawyer made a hiccuping gasp. "Don't use my words against me!"

"Not trying to. But it's true. I don't know what this is going to do. I wanted to talk to you first, but I'm not asking your permission. This is my decision."

"This is all *because* of me. Don't you get it?"

Nick snorted. "Sawyer, I don't care if you're some goddess's son or if you're Captain Underpants. This is not all about you."

"But—"

"Bullshit. Cut it out. I have more stuff to tell you."

Sawyer apparently flopped over on someone, because Nick heard a distinctive male grunt from the other end of the phone. "Tell me."

"Who'd you squish?"

"Saeward. It's fine. Tell me."

"That's the big one, right?"

"Yeah. Hippocamp."

"What's that?"

"Don't try to distract me," Sawyer complained.

"I'm not. I don't know what that is."

"Sea creature. He's sort of half-man, half-horse, half-merman. But he's not a merman."

"So he's a sea horse?"

Sawyer sighed, and he heard a grumble from the other end of the phone. "That's why I say merman, Ward! It's the visual! And no, Nick. Not a sea horse. Except, yeah. A giant seahorse. Sort of."

"You don't make sense."

"Yeah, well, neither do you. Tell me the rest, Nick. Stop stalling."

Nick wandered into the bedroom and stretched out on the messy bed. Jedrek's scent was stronger there. He needed it. "I guess I'm an alpha. I have a pack."

"What?"

"Yeah. I don't know. Remember the lady with the lion cubs?"

"Holy shit."

"Yeah. But see, they wanted to do the magic spell on her instead, 'cause the magic is newer. Sawyer, I can't let them do that. She's got babies, you know? But we need to find out who did this, because if they were still pulling this bullshit three years ago, they could still be pulling it now. I need to find out."

Sawyer made another of his sounds, this one closer to a meep, and Nick could practically hear his brain working. "Okay. I don't like this.

But I'll never like it. And Henry's told me how much he trusts Zaire. And how strong Keziah's coven is. So... you have the best people with you to help. I'll have Draco bring me—"

"No."

"Nick—"

"No. We don't know what the hell is going to happen, Sawyer. You being here will only stress me out. Besides, I kind of have a mate now, too. He'll be with me."

Sawyer gasped, and Nick heard another oomph of pain from Ward. "What? You didn't *lead* with that!"

Nick grinned. "I saved the best for last."

"Who? When? How? Tell me."

"Jedrek. Pretty much day one. You know how. We fucked. A lot. Some biting happened."

"The giant Viking hellhound is your mate. This is epic."

"I think so. He's kinda mad at me at the moment. So there's that."

Sawyer sighed and flopped back down on Saeward. Nick probably should apologize to the poor guy. Sawyer was all knees and elbows when he was upset. "He doesn't want you to do the spell."

"Probably not. But he knows it's the right thing to do, too. Tell me another way. One that doesn't put a mother and her babies at risk. Because I can't think of one."

"You're strong," Sawyer said quietly. "And an alpha. Henry's brothers and sisters... I mean, they could try with them, too. But that thought makes me want to throw up, you know?"

"Yeah. I thought about it for like two seconds. I'm the best one."

"I know. But I kinda wanna throw up at that thought, too."

Nick gave Sawyer another minute to process. Just listened to him breathing on the other end of the phone. His brother was the smart one, even had a fancy master's degree to prove it. "Hey, I have a question."

"What?"

"What was Mama Thea?" Sawyer made a squeaking noise. "I mean, she got three of us from this world, you know? And I remember now from when she found me that she helped me shift back to human. She was something."

"I don't know," Sawyer said. "Holy crap."

"Yeah. But I think Papa Smith was human."

Sawyer hummed, thinking it over. "That makes sense. I mean, I guess he could have been something different. There are so many creatures out there, Nick. More than you can imagine."

"I get that. But I'm thinking human."

"What a fairy tale," Sawyer said. "The beautiful fairy princess meets her human white knight and falls in love. But she has to give up her powers and immortality to be with him. But she does it. And then she finds three misfit orphans and keeps them safe."

"Sounds like something she'd do."

"Yeah," Sawyer agreed. "I'll ask Mother next time I see her, okay?"

"Okay. So I'm gonna go. I want to go track down Jedrek. He's been gone long enough."

"Nick?"

"Yeah?"

"I love you. Please be safe. And make sure you call me when it's done. I'll worry and show up there if you don't."

"I will. And, ya know. Love you, too."

Nick ended the call and rolled onto his side. He couldn't deny that talking to Sawyer and getting his support made him feel a little better. But he still wanted Jedrek's okay as well. It itched beneath his skin, knowing his mate was upset and he'd been the one to cause it. Nick didn't know what to do to fix it, though.

He heard footsteps on the porch, then the door burst open. He didn't know what to do, but Nick had a sneaking suspicion that he was about to find out. Jedrek stomped into the bedroom, his eyes blazing with the fire of the hellhound. He growled.

"Nice."

Jedrek flung off his shirt and tugged at his pants. He was naked a second later.

"Nicer."

Jedrek pounced, rolling Nick onto his back and straddling his waist.

Nick groaned. "Nicest."

"There are ground rules," Jedrek growled.

"If by ground rules you mean the lube is on the ground right there and you should probably get it, then yes. Ground rules."

Jedrek growled. But he reached down and grabbed the lube anyway. Then he leaned forward and pressed his forehead into Nick's.

"Tell me," Nick said softly. He couldn't resist touching, all Jedrek's beautiful skin and rippling muscles right there for him to explore. He stroked Jedrek's sides, over his ribs. Down again, over his hips then to the curve of his ass.

"Don't be stupid. Listen to Keziah and the others."

"Agreed."

"Don't be stupid."

"Got it."

"I can't think when you're touching me," Jedrek complained.

"I can stop."

"Don't you dare."

Nick grinned and moved his head. He found Jedrek's lips with his and teased them. "I wouldn't dream of it."

He deepened the kiss, swallowing all of Jedrek's anger and fear then replacing it with all the emotions rolling inside of him. He didn't have words, had never had them where Jedrek was concerned. They just were. From the moment he'd seen him, shifted and out of control at his apartment. This stranger had become part of his soul. His grounding. His foundation. His safety. And Jedrek couldn't know how much he'd changed Nick's life. He'd found the missing pieces. His lion and his mate. He couldn't do any of this without both of them.

"Stop thinking," Jedrek rumbled.

His lion moved inside him, agreeing completely with Jedrek's sentiments. And Nick got it, finally. A moment of clarity. He didn't need to tell Jedrek. He needed to show him. His instincts went into overdrive and he poured heat and need into the kiss. Jedrek moved above him, grinding down, desperately seeking more. Nick growled and flipped them over, leaving Jedrek panting on his back, flame-filled eyes demanding.

"Nick, please."

He couldn't resist the call. Anything Jedrek wanted was his. And what he wanted was Nick. He grabbed the lube and slicked himself up, never taking his eyes from Jedrek's. Just that much, that simple, penetrating look, was more intimate than anything they'd done before. He saw it all in Jedrek's eyes, his future in the fire.

Nick ran his hands slowly up Jedrek's thighs before moving up further. He held himself in position, cock poised at Jedrek's entrance.

Jedrek reached between them and guided Nick's cock to his hole. He pushed, slowly, his cock sliding through Jedrek's fingers and into his body. And still, he looked. Chased the flames of desire even as they burned brighter. Even as he moved deeper and sealed them together, so far into Jedrek that he could feel his heartbeat. He leaned closer, began to move his hips. Jedrek's breath caught, and something in his eyes changed.

"What is it?" Nick asked. His voice barely there, so locked into his mate that he didn't dare break the spell they were under.

Jedrek tugged him closer until they were pressed chest to chest and their breaths intermingled. "Don't be stupid," Jedrek repeated once more.

He sounded so desperate, so worried. Outside of his brothers, Nick hadn't had anyone worry for him, be scared for him. Hell, he didn't even have anyone who worried whether or not he ate his vegetables.

"What?" Jedrek asked.

"Are you going to make me eat broccoli?"

The look he got was priceless. Then Jedrek laughed, wrapped his legs more tightly around Nick's waist, and squeezed. Every inch of

Nick felt cradled, adored. Nick sighed and tucked his face into Jedrek's neck. He slowly moved, sliding his cock out and in again, drawing a surprised gasp from his mate.

"I'll make you eat broccoli. Or I won't. Whatever you want. As long as you don't stop."

Nick thrust harder, driving deeper into Jedrek while nipping at his neck. He inhaled Jedrek's scent, loved the sweetness of them merging together, their scents so combined that he couldn't separate them. "I hate broccoli," Nick gasped.

Jedrek's hole clenched around him and he began to move as well, his hips pushing back, meeting each thrust. "Then I won't make you."

He made the promise as he arched his neck to the side, baring it to Nick's hungry gaze. He bit down, unable to resist, and Jedrek clenched him tighter, held him closer.

"Fuck me," Jedrek demanded.

Nick growled and bit down harder. Jedrek cried out and rubbed his cock frantically against Nick's abs as he continued thrusting into him. His body heated, screaming for release. But not until his mate was satisfied. Not until his mate knew his intentions were pure and true.

And Jedrek, of course he knew. He held Nick's head, encouraged him to keep his teeth in Jedrek's neck. He owned him. Nick may be the one with teeth in Jedrek's neck, but every piece of Nick was his. And that moment, that realization, that he'd given this hellhound all of him, was enough to send him over the edge. He tried to fight back, tried to change his angle and make it better but Jedrek wouldn't let him. He squeezed his legs and Nick lost his mind. He came, all thoughts going to his cock and filling his mate with his seed, his scent marking him, claiming him. Jed was his. No others. Never.

Jedrek yelled, tightening around him until Nick couldn't move his cock. He fucked him though his release, waiting until he unclenched before raising his head. The flames were still there, burning bright. Jedrek tugged him to the side, moving Nick around until he was in his usual spot, using Jedrek as his body pillow. He laid his head on Jedrek's shoulder and closed his eyes.

He could feel the nervous tension still there, bubbling beneath the surface, but he couldn't pretend he wasn't nervous as well. But he had plenty to fight for, and no matter what the magic brought, he wasn't going to let Jedrek go. He had a pack now, a life, and even if he had no idea how it had happened, even if rationally he should be more lost than ever, he'd never been more grounded. He wasn't going to lose control or fly apart at the seams. He couldn't. He had a mate depending on him, and people could say a lot of things about Nick, but he'd never been accused of being stupid. He had too much shit to figure out, and he found himself looking forward to doing it with his big lug of a hellhound at his side.

NICK

It was strange going back to that same circle of stones where they'd arrived. It was stranger that he was wearing a weird long white robe. He looked like fucking Princess Leia. If only he had a blaster and those weird donut hair buns. At least he could be sure it wasn't because he was some sacrificial virgin. One, he and Jedrek alone had made sure he was nice and impure. So, so impure. Two, Keziah and the rest of the coven were wearing the same white robes. Apparently it was important to the ritual. He knew jack shit about rituals.

The wards keeping people out were as strong as ever at the circle. Keziah explained that's why he wanted to do the spell there. It was well-warded and outside of their home. If things went badly, whatever they unleashed would be contained. Leandra and the kids were just inside the wards. She looked about as happy as Jedrek did with his decision. Even though no one had said anything, Leandra had probably figured out that he was taking her place. She wasn't an idiot.

"We are not having a moment right now. You hear me?" Nick complained.

"What? You expect me to declare my undying love or something?"

Nick grunted.

She grinned. "Kick their ass."

"That's my plan. Here. Hold my beer."

He didn't have a beer, but she got the joke and grinned back at him.

"It's probably best if you take the kids back."

"Probably."

"You aren't going to listen to me, are you?"

"Nope. You might need us. Your pack may be small, but we're mighty."

Nick grinned and ran his fingers over Ariella's cheek. She had pudding all over it. The little monster. "That we are. If there's trouble—"

"I'll get them out of danger, but we'll help if we can."

Nick grunted. "Back in a few."

He went to the circle of rocks and scowled. It looked like a scene out of some chick flick horror movie combo. Flower petals and candles yet circle of rocks in the middle of dark woods with strange robe-wearing witches. "Seriously?"

Keziah grinned. "Shut up and get in the circle."

"You should at least buy me dinner first."

"I made you breakfast. And gave you my sausage ball recipe."

"Fair point."

Still, Nick hovered nervously outside the rocks.

Jedrek stepped up behind him, wrapping his arms around Nick's waist. Warm breath ghosted over his neck and he closed his eyes.

"I'll be right here," Jedrek promised.

"Yeah."

Nick opened his eyes. Zaire hovered on the opposite side of the circle, clearly as nervous as Nick. But also as determined. She nodded her head, and somehow that was what he needed. He stepped

GIVE HIM HELL 171

forward into the circle, leaving the safety of Jedrek's arms, and faced Keziah.

"You sure you know what you're doing?"

"No clue. But I trust my magic."

Good enough for him. He turned to Calder next. The ice had started to melt with the water elemental, but he still didn't completely trust Nick. Nick liked that about him.

"You ready?"

"Yes."

"Good."

Next, Rowan, who looked nervous. "It's not too late to say you aren't ready."

"I'm ready," Rowan said. "Just a little scared. Is stage fright a thing when magic is concerned?"

"I'd say just imagine me naked, but well, you've already seen that."

"I can still imagine it," Rowan teased.

Some of the nervous tension eased. Rowan pulled in a breath and smiled, so Nick made the final turn.

Emmett stood tall, but Nick could sense his unease. "You up for this?"

"I'm fine."

"Not what I asked," Nick snarled. "Are. You. Up. For. This?"

Emmett scowled. "Yes."

"Good. When this is over, you and I are having a little chat. And you're not going to like what I have to say."

"I don't like you," Emmett snapped. "But I'm going to help you anyway."

Nick turned one last time, facing Keziah again.

They stared at each other for a long moment.

"I won't let you down," Keziah whispered.

"Never doubted it for a second. Let's get this party started."

Keziah nodded and raised his arms. The coven joined hands, forming a circle around Nick. And Nick, he turned his attention to

Jedrek, standing stoic and true on the other side of the rocks. So close Nick could almost touch him, but a world away. None of that mattered, though. All he needed to see was Jedrek's eyes. Fire and smoke. His mate was so ticked off. It was beautiful to see. He was ready for answers, too. The only reason Nick was getting away with this nonsense was because they all wanted answers. Jedrek had a few scores to settle with the asshats who'd hurt Ben and Henry. He wanted to tear a few new holes in the ones who gave Jack and Emily nightmares. He wanted blood for the pieces of shit who had Natasha desperate to know how to protect herself from danger. And he wanted to kill them for forcing six-year-old Ollie to escape through a hole in the roof and run into the night to find help, to save them all from certain death. Yeah, Jedrek was pissed alright. And now, because of them, Nick was in danger. Nick grinned, even as he felt the magic swirling around him as the coven chanted. His mate was stunningly beautiful when he was pissed off.

Jedrek met his gaze, cocked one eyebrow. Then he grinned back. Feral. Dangerous. Deadly.

The lion stirred. Magic poked at him and he snarled.

Nick tried to keep the other side of him calm. *Steady. Control. Breathe.*

Jedrek sucked in a long breath, then let it out. Nick mimicked him.

The magic jabbed against him. The lion snarled again.

Danger. Threat. Attack.

Nick breathed.

The magic intensified. Stabbing into him.

Nick flinched.

The lion roared.

Just breathe.

Jedrek's eyes deepened, embers so hot they'd almost changed to white. Fascinating. Beautiful. Mate.

The lion swatted against him, batting the magic away, but Nick held. Breathed. And when it stabbed again, the lion bled.

Nick gasped, pain deep in his side.

Jedrek stepped forward, but Nick held up his hand. Claws formed, then receded.

The magic stabbed him again, and the lion howled his rage. He'd fight this. Fight it to the death.

Nick breathed.

The lion bled. So much blood. And Nick realized what had to happen. He thought about what he'd learned from Leandra, the stories the other kids had told. The way their magic was so tangled up inside. The way his had been dark, so dark when Mama Thea found him that she'd thought it best to lock it away to keep him safe.

It wasn't natural. He wasn't supposed to have this beast in him. It wasn't his. He met Jedrek's gaze, his eyes golden. For the last time. He dropped to his knees, no longer able to hold himself up. The lion fought, but he didn't stand a chance. Not against the coven. The most powerful coven. The only thing stronger than him. Something dripped down Nick's face, and he broke eye contact with Jedrek for the first time. Blood dotted the white robes.

Jedrek roared.

Nick lifted his head, meeting his mate's gaze once more.

Steady. Breathe. *Jedrek.*

Jedrek ran forward, but he couldn't penetrate the wards.

He tasted the blood now and wiped his mouth.

"Nick!"

He smiled. He probably was a gruesome mess. Leandra appeared at Jedrek's shoulders. Her eyes blazed yellow. The cubs' did, too. Nick's own faded. He drooped to the side.

"Got it," Rowan shouted.

Nick really needed a nap.

"Holy shit. Nick!"

Keziah dropped to his knees beside him, and the rest of the coven joined him a moment later. He felt their hands on him, but he kept his eyes on his pack. No, not his anymore. They couldn't be. A cool rush of magic washed over him, soothing the ache. The stabbing had receded with the lion, but Nick wouldn't pretend it didn't hurt. He had a gaping hole inside him now, but it wasn't one anyone could see. Hell, he shouldn't even care. He'd spent the last fourteen years not even understanding what he was. He was back to that now. But he wasn't giving them up. Not Jedrek. Never. And not Leandra and the kids either. They needed a family. Someone to count on. And Nick was reliable. He was good at being family. His brothers would back him up on that. So what if he wasn't their alpha anymore. He didn't want to be an alpha anyway. It was fine.

The coven continued to work their magic, and the pain left completely. Nick wiped his face once more, surprised to find it wet with tears. "Well, shit."

"Let me in," Jedrek demanded. "Now."

Keziah lowered the wards and Jedrek was at his side a moment later. Leandra knelt too, lowering the kids to the ground. Ariella patted his hair, Lionel kicked him in the shoulder. The little stinker. Nick growled... except it really wasn't a growl anymore.

Leandra sniffed and lowered her head to his. Jedrek had his hand, squeezed it too tight, but Nick didn't care. He needed the connection.

"Did it work?" Nick asked.

"Yeah. I found it." Rowan turned to Emmett, who had closed his eyes. They seemed to share something, one of those magic things Nick didn't know shit about, but Emmett opened them again a second later. "I see it. I know where to go."

"Damn straight you do. Jedrek, open one of those flamey circle things. Let's go kick some ass."

Jedrek scowled at him. "You're hurt."

"No, I'm not. I'm fine."

Jedrek growled.

"Lion?" Ariella asked.

"No, little bit. I'm not a lion anymore. But I'm still your Nick."

"Nick! Nick!" Lionel grabbed his hair and used it as a lever to climb onto Nick's head.

Leandra gasped out a sob, but Nick reached for her hand. "I'm glad it was me and not you."

"Dammit, Nick."

"Totally worth it. If we catch these sons of bitches, then I have zero regrets."

"We can," Emmett said. "We need to go, though."

"Not we," Zaire said. "You four aren't going anywhere. Stay in the circle. Close it up. I taught you better than this. Jedrek, get your mate."

"We can help," Keziah said.

"No, you can't. And before you argue, I'm not being a bitch, son. I'm speaking the truth. You did your part. Now we're going to do ours and call the alpha of the hellhounds and bring him in. If he needs you, he'll decide that. That's our job. That is the duty of the awen and the coven."

Nick pulled Lionel off his head and passed him back to Leandra. "Well, I'm coming."

Jedrek growled.

"Snarl all you want, big guy. But I deserve this. I started this fight, and I'm going to be there when it's finished."

Nick didn't fight it when Jedrek pulled him up. He led him out of the circle then pulled Nick close. He breathed, but his breath caught. "I know. I smell different. But I'm still yours. Right?"

"Mine," Jedrek rumbled.

Nick let out a sigh of relief. He'd been a smidge worried.

He heard the familiar whoosh as a portal opened. He lifted his head, smiled at his mate, and then turned to face the alpha. Solomon stepped through with Calli at his side. They both stared.

"Guess what we found?" Nick said.

Solomon stared him down, frowning with unease. "What happened to you?"

"They needed magic to find the bastards we're looking for. I gave 'em mine."

Calli gasped. "What?"

Nick shrugged. "I hadn't used it for a long time. I'm glad I got to see what it was like for a while. But it had to be done. Now, can we go kick some ass?"

"Nick—"

"Jedrek, I will not fuck you for a month if the next words out of your mouth are anything but let's go."

Jedrek growled and pulled him close.

Solomon turned to Keziah, who had managed to close the circle. He hovered near his coven, the four of them sticking close. "Keziah?"

"I can show you," Emmett said. He grabbed Keziah's hand, and Solomon touched Keziah's head.

Solomon's eyes blazed, and then settled again before he grinned ferally. "Let's go get ourselves a witch."

He opened another portal. Nick and Jedrek stepped forward. Jedrek tugged him in for a kiss, then grabbed Nick's hand in his. "Stay behind me."

"Sure."

Jedrek growled but pulled him along anyway. They reappeared outside a nice little cottage in the woods. It could have been out of a fairy tale. An old lady opened the door and stepped outside. She glared at them, but Solomon stepped forward, eyes blazing, and her face fell. "I didn't think you'd find us."

"Yeah," Solomon said. "But we did. Where is she?"

Nick had a sneaking suspicion he knew exactly which *she* hid inside. *Mrs. Foote.* He wanted to tear her throat out with his teeth. Except he couldn't do that anymore. Maybe Jedrek would do it for him.

"Here."

Nick could have passed her on the street a million times and never recognized her. But he knew that voice. Cold and deadly. But the outside didn't match what he remembered at all. She'd not been old, then. And it hadn't been that long. But she was a crone now, wrinkled and hunched. She even walked with a cane. She looked... fragile.

"And here I thought you'd never find me."

"Gwen!" The other lady didn't seem impressed by Gwen— Mrs. Foote's— snarly attitude. Nick couldn't say he was either. He was surprised she had a name. Which, you know, of all things to be surprised about, was pretty stupid. The others seemed more upset by her tone.

Solomon growled. "Alpha Jerrick killed you."

She scoffed. "You don't think he'd let me off that easily, do you? Now why don't you go back where you came from before you give me fleas, dog."

Calli and Jedrek snarled. Jedrick took a step forward and growled.

"Oh, the puppies think they scare me? I've faced worse. Much worse. And survived."

Nick wanted her dead. He clenched his fists. He really, really wanted her dead.

Jedrek lost control and bolted forward.

"Jed!" Nick barked his mate's name. Jedrek skidded to a stop. He'd half-shifted, ready to get vengeance on Nick's behalf. Nick knew it. He felt it. Saw the anger on Jedrek's face. But Nick would be damned if he gave her what she wanted.

Even Solomon seemed surprised. Nick stepped forward.

"You want this, don't you?" Nick asked. Jedrek touched his arm, but Nick didn't take his eyes off her. "You want it to be easy, quick. You've been praying for this, haven't you? Wishing from the crusty, black depths of your heart that they'd find you once more. End this for you. Give you the easy way out."

She turned to him, hatred so deep in her eyes. "And who are you?"

"I believe you called me Lion. My family calls me Nick."

She glared. "You aren't a lion."

Nick grinned. She flinched. "I gave it up so I could have this moment. But now... I don't know. I think I have it wrong. I don't know shit about all this, but I think... I think there's something you fear worse than them."

She snarled. "I remember you now. Sniveling brat. Always close to the tigers and the little bear. I killed her, you know. She was so weak. Jenny. Wasn't that what you called her? And poor, poor Max. I took care of him not long after you left them. He cried for days. Begged for you to come save him. I put him out of his misery."

Nick swallowed back the bile in his throat. He glanced at Jedrek, arched a brow. Jedrek growled, willing to do what Nick wanted. He'd reward him for that later. Much, much later. Well, maybe not too much. He had *needs*. Nick turned to Solomon. "Jedrek told me a story. About how you guys take creatures who abuse their roles here to the goddess for judgment."

Solomon grinned. "We do."

"I don't know anyone who deserves judgment more than this piece of shit, do you?"

"No, Nick. No, I don't."

"And see, I think she has a few more secrets left in her. Secrets she is so afraid will come out. She's more afraid of that than anything. She wants to die so she won't tell. But I think... I think a goddess could get the truth out of her. What do you guys think?"

Solomon stepped forward and grabbed her by the shoulders. "I like the way you think."

A portal opened directly behind her and he shoved her through. She screamed in terror, but Solomon followed. Calli drew her sword and held it at the neck of the other witch as Nick stepped forward, too. Jedrek grabbed his hand and they walked through their second portal of the night. Together.

"I'm going to take this one to Zaire," Calli said. "I have a few questions."

"See you soon," Jedrek nodded.

The portal closed behind them, and Nick found himself in a curious patch of forest. Everything here was quiet, not alive like the woods he'd spent the past week running through with Jedrek and

Leandra. He would miss that most, those moments of peace with them at his side. But they'd figure out a new way.

He tightened his hold on Jedrek's hand. Then he gulped. "Holy shit. Is she going to come?"

Jedrek grinned. "That's how this works."

Solomon had Mrs. Foote on her knees on the ground. He held onto her head, not taking any chances. Nick wasn't sure how he felt about it all, but he didn't have time to process. The forest came alive and began to glow. Sound returned and with it power. So much power Nick could hardly breathe. He closed his eyes. Jedrek pulled him in, tucked Nick's face in his neck.

"Breathe."

Just breathe.

Jedrek guided him down onto his knees, but he kept Nick wrapped in his arms.

"Goddesses," Solomon whispered.

"What have you brought us?"

Damn. Even her voice had power. Nick wanted to look, but Jedrek held him steady. Probably not a good idea for a mere human to look upon a goddess. He'd probably vaporize or something.

"We finally found her, my goddess. The one who used her magic against the cubs so long ago."

A burst of angry magic pounded against him and Nick tightened his hold on Jedrek.

"Easy, sister."

Another voice, this one as fierce and powerful as the first.

"Show me," the first goddess said.

Nick had no idea what that meant, but after a second he felt her magic again. So weird. He wanted to look, dammit.

And then he got his chance.

JEDREK

J edrek held Nick to him and waited for the goddesses to decide the fate of the woman who'd hurt so many of the people he loved. The kids— Goddess, they deserved this. They deserved to know the monster who'd hurt them for so long was gone. And Nick. Jedrek couldn't believe that he'd fallen head over heels for a stubborn lion— human. Nick was human now. But just as strong and fierce as he'd been before. It was good to know those traits weren't the lion's alone.

"Jedrek."

He raised his head, eyes damp. He hadn't even realized he'd been crying. Couldn't, in fact, remember the last time he'd shed a tear. "Yes, my goddess."

"Come to me. Bring your mate."

Jedrek nodded. He gave Nick one last squeeze before letting him go. He rose then pulled Nick to his feet. Nick hadn't opened his eyes. "It's okay, Simba. You can look now."

Nick opened his eyes and glared. "Ass."

Jedrek grinned. "Your ass."

Nick poked him in the ribs.

Instead of retaliating, Jedrek wrapped his arm around Nick's shoulders and turned him to face the goddesses. Only two of the three sisters were present. Their fire goddess and the earth goddess. She hadn't taken her eyes off Nick from the moment he turned around. And Mrs. Foote, well, she'd vanished. Last he'd looked, both goddesses had hands on her, and then... nothing. Jedrek hoped she burned in hell.

Jedrek guided them closer and Nick didn't seem to know where to look.

"This is some crazy shit. I mean, uh. Stuff. Shit. I mean. Dammit."

Jedrek laughed. The goddesses did as well.

"Such language. I believe he thinks we have not heard it before, sister."

Nick groaned. "Sorry. It's been a really crazy couple of weeks."

The earth goddess stepped closer. She held out her hand to Nick. "May I?"

"Uh, may you what?"

"See."

Jedrek leaned in. "She can see your memories of the last few weeks. She wants to see from your eyes what happened."

Nick made the strangest face Jedrek had ever seen. "Uh, that's cool and all but, uh... see, I just sort of met this guy this week, and well, things happened. Really, really good things. But private things. And, you know. Look. I'll just say it. Orgasms. Lots of orgasms happened. And that's not something I care to share, okay?"

Jedrek thought the gates might open and swallow him down into hell.

Solomon choked and started cackling. The goddess did as well. Nick's goddess, on the other hand, simply looked smug.

"You think I've not heard it before?"

"Oh, come on. That's just...wrong."

She grinned. "I will not look at the private times between you and your mate. You have my word."

Nick glanced at Jedrek, a question in his eyes.

"It's good."

He turned back to her and shrugged. "Okay. Just don't be surprised at how many times I thought about lube over the past week."

Jedrek groaned and the goddess reached out and touched Nick's head. Her eyes glowed a stunning emerald green and within seconds, it was done. She stepped away and sniffed, wiping a single tear from her cheek. "You are a true champion, son of Xsayarsa."

"Son of what now?"

She grinned. "Tell me... Nick, I believe you are called in this realm... how did you decide to set the lion free?"

"I don't know." Nick shrugged. "I just figured... everything that happened, you know. It was all fucked-up magic. And even though it fought me— Damn, did that lion fight me— when the coven was doing their thing, it wasn't messing with me. It was messing with him. So I figured they needed whatever it was making me lion. That was the dark magic. I'm worried about the other kids, though. What this means for them."

"And what would you say to those kids, Nick? Would you tell them how evil the animal inside is? How dark it is?"

Nick scoffed. "No. You kiddin' me? The lion wasn't fucked up. It was good. But there was dark magic attached. Hell, I don't know shit about this stuff but—"

"You know more than you think. Your instincts speak to you, strongly, and you have the gift of listening. It is a great power."

Nick gave her a look like she was off her rocker and Jedrek coughed to get his attention. He widened his eyes, trying to remind Nick to be respectful, but Nick just shrugged again.

"It's not that great of a power. I mean, look at these guys. Portals and flames and shifting with their pants on. That's powerful shit right there."

The goddess gave him a quizzical look, then glanced at her sister.

"He seems to want to be one of yours, sister. I believe he meets the qualifications."

Jedrek nearly choked. He grabbed Nick from behind. Held him close. He couldn't believe his—

"Whoa, whoa, whoa," Nick said. "If you're saying what I think you're saying, thanks but no thanks. I mean, I love my mate and all—"

Jedrek choked again and held him closer.

"— Oh, yeah. Sorry Jedrek but I mean, come on. I think this is love, right? I don't know shit about love but man, I can't imagine a single day without you. The thought of it makes me crazy. And you're clearly the most beautiful man on the planet. I mean shit, so fucking hot. And don't get me started on the coolness factor of the hellhound. What's not to love? Well, I mean, except your inability to cook. We need to work on that." Nick turned to look at his goddess. "Could you maybe help us out? Because we might starve. It's a problem."

He'd never seen his goddess look more stunned.

"I... I..."

"Yeah, it's too weird, right? I get it." Nick turned back to the earth goddess. "But as I was saying, I appreciate the offer, but I'm fine being human. I think it'd be weird to have someone else as my alpha, now that I was one, you know? It doesn't feel right."

She smiled at him.

"I have someone who would very much like to see you."

"Yeah?"

The goddess waved her fingers around and the trees parted. A lion walked through them. A very familiar lion. Jedrek gasped, squeezing Nick a little too hard in the process.

"Dude. Is that... that's..."

The lion prowled forward coming closer to Nick before head butting him in the chest. Nick knelt in front of him and grabbed the lion's face. "I'm so sorry. I didn't want to hurt you. You know I didn't. But dammit, they're hurting kids. And I don't want to think about what they're doing to Leandra and the other mothers. It kills me to think there are more out there. I had to stop them, right? Someone hurts our pride, we hurt them."

The lion threw back its head and roared. Jedrek couldn't believe his eyes. Nick had tears flowing down his cheeks but he stayed strong, kneeling there in front of the beast.

The goddess touched the lion's head and smiled. "You speak to him as if he is not you, but you are wrong, Nick. He is you. You cut away half of your soul to save the others, let half of you be stripped away. But I offer you this boon in return. I can return your other half to you, if that is your wish. But I'm afraid if I grant you this, I must ask for something else in return."

"It's what I want most, after Jedrek," Nick said. "But it feels like a trap."

"Not a trap. May I?" She held out her hand again.

"No funny business," Nick warned. But he leaned closer and let her touch his head.

Nick swayed and when she removed her hand, he fell back against Jedrek. He looked to the lion, then back at her. "Are you sure about this?"

"Yes."

"Then you have a deal."

She grinned and reached out once more. Jedrek looked on in shock and amazement as her magic flowed around them, trees and leaves circling them until suddenly he couldn't see where Nick ended and the lion began. And then, there weren't two of them anymore. There was only Nick, who turned in his arms and looked up at him with glowing golden eyes.

Jedrek couldn't resist. He pulled him in and kissed him like he'd never kissed him before. Nick growled and jumped, wrapping his legs around Jedrek's waist.

The goddesses both laughed, and the sound was the only thing that brought Nick up for air.

"Probably should have talked to you first. This is gonna be... crazy sauce."

"I trust you."

Nick grinned and kissed him again.

The goddess cleared her throat.

"Son of Xsayarsa, you have your mission, but we have learned a great deal more from this foul excuse of a witch than simply the worst of her evil deeds."

"Wow, that sounded like a line from a really bad movie."

Jedrek groaned and pushed Nick away. "Behave."

"What? It did."

"Nick," Solomon said, "Focus."

"Oh. Yeah. Sorry. I'm kinda buzzed at the moment. Ready to get to work." He glanced at Jedrek again. "Really should have talked to you first."

Jedrek grabbed his hand. "We'll deal with it."

"That's not all we must deal with," the fire goddess said.

"Our brother is behind this. He used his abilities to manipulate magic. He is trying to gain power, enough power to defeat Sawyer and prevent him from fulfilling the prophesy."

"I knew it," Nick said. "He's totally the air god, or whatever, isn't he?"

She looked at him, a blank stare, and then nodded. Jedrek thought every bit of air had been sucked away from him. "What?"

"I told you," Nick said. "There should be four. There's four elements. Fire." he pointed at Jedrek's goddess. "Earth." He pointed to his. "The water one. And air. Just like the coven. One was missing. Remember? I thought it might be the mother but that didn't make any sense. Except... wait... what does that make Sawyer?"

The goddesses shared a look. "Our brother is something else. We are forbidden from speaking of this."

"Of course you are. Does Sawyer know?"

They shared another look.

"So we're about to have, holy shit, it's like the Titan wars or some shit. What was it called?"

Nick turned to him, but Jedrek didn't have a clue. His mind was still reeling over the realignment of the deities as he'd known them for as long as… "I don't know."

"Well, remember that movie? It was so bad. Battle of the gods, or some shit. The younger generation basically fought it out with the older ones. That's how Zeus became king of the gods or whatever. Holy shit, is Sawyer Zeus? Can he like throw lightning bolts and shit?"

"No."

"Oh."

The wind had clearly been knocked out of Nick's sails. Jedrek looked at Solomon, who seemed just as confused as he felt.

"What do we do?" Jedrek asked.

"You already have your tasks," his goddess replied. "But beware. Our brother is devious. And now that he's lost his only source of power, he will be desperate."

"Lost his power?" Solomon asked.

"Yeah," Nick replied. "I've got that one. Will explain later. At least tell me you took care of that… woman. Because I want to tell Ben he can sleep tonight, you know? He deserves to know she's gone forever."

Both goddesses came toward him, and Nick stood tall. Jedrek had never wanted him more.

"She is gone forever. You have our word. And now we know all of those who helped her. My hellhounds have a new task of their own."

Solomon grinned. "Happy to serve."

"Good. We must work fast. Time is of the essence. Nick, you know what to do?"

"Yes, my goddess."

She smiled. "You will serve me well, my champion."

Before Jedrek could even process it all, they were gone.

Nick turned in his arms and then he had his mate wrapped around him.

"Holy shit. That was either the coolest thing ever, or the weirdest dream ever. I don't… I don't know which one I want it to be."

"What do we need to do, Nick?" Solomon asked.

"First, I need to speak to my brother. Privately. But then I need..." Nick paused and cocked his head to the side, as if listening. "I need Ben. And Ollie. Can you bring them to our place?"

Solomon glanced at Jedrek, questioning, but he shrugged. He had no idea what was going on either.

"Sure," Solomon said. He opened a portal, and after sending Jedrek one last look, he left.

Jedrek stood alone with his mate in front of the gates. Nick looked up at him, his golden eyes back again.

"I can't believe that just happened."

"No shit. What was all that Son of the X-man stuff."

"Xsayarsa," Jedrek said.

"Like that helps me."

"Xsayarsa is the king of the lions."

"Oh. How do you know that?"

Jedrek shrugged. He'd been around for a while.

"Wait, does that mean he's like... my dad?"

Jedrek grinned and leaned their foreheads together. "No. Just means you're in the lion clan."

"Oh. Yeah, that makes sense."

"So...you planning on telling me what you signed us up for?"

Nick grinned. "Sawyer first. He's probably worried himself sick."

"Okay. Let's go."

Jedrek opened a portal. As much as he wanted to know, he didn't mind letting Nick handle it his way. He took them just outside the wards then waited for the vampires to do their security duty.

Nick looked around in amazement. "Whoa. He wasn't kidding when he said it was a McMansion."

"It's probably not big enough. I think they underestimated."

Nick looked at him like he had two heads. "That's not big enough?"

"He has eight mates. And a staff. And security."

"You might have a point. He'll make it work, though. Sawyer

wouldn't be comfortable living in some big mansion place. This is probably making him itch."

"I'll ask him. He's running down the hill like his ass is on fire."

Nick ran forward, too, but bumped against the wards. He snarled at them. And the wards dropped. Nick seemed incredibly pleased with himself, but Jedrek noticed Henry at the top of the hill. He waved, and the mage waved back. Sawyer skidded to a stop at Nick's side. "Well? What happened? Did it work?"

"It worked. Why'd you run all the way down here like an idiot? I'm hungry. I wanted food. Jedrek can't cook, and you know I can't. I even asked the goddess if she'd help, but she was like, uh, no. So I figured, my brother has a fancy chef and a butler, the least he can do is get me dinner."

Sawyer's mouth fell open and he stared at Nick like he'd lost his mind. At least it wasn't just him.

"You...met the goddess."

"Yeah. Come on, Sawyer. I'm hungry. Hey, you'll feed Jedrek, too, right? 'Cause, you know, he's my mate and all so if he's hungry and I eat, that's just... well."

"Why are you being so weird?" Sawyer asked. "You're hyper. Are you high?"

"Buzzed," Nick confessed. "A little hyper. So much. Come on. Feed me."

"Okay."

Sawyer gave Jedrek a look, but he had no clue how to interpret it. He simply followed the brothers up to the big house, and then through to the kitchen. Jedrek had met Viv a couple times and she waved at him before turning to the Smith brothers. "Sawyer," she said cooly. Uh-oh. Sawyer was obviously in trouble.

"Viv," Sawyer said. "Come on. I explained this already. Stop being mad at me. My brother is hungry."

Viv turned to Nick. "Well aren't you a cool drink of water on a hot day."

Nick blinked. "I have no idea what that means."

"She means you're hot, Nick."

"Oh, I have a mate. Sorry."

"Damn," Viv said. "Fine. Go somewhere else. I'll make food."

"I'll wait here," Jedrek said.

Nick nodded before looping his head around Sawyer's neck and dragging him out of the room. "Dude, goddesses. I met your sisters. Weird. Does that make them my step-sisters? Oh, are they evil step-sisters? Nah, they were nice."

His voice drifted away and Jedrek turned back to Viv with a smile. "They're both maniacs."

"Pretty much. So he's yours?"

"Guilty as charged," Jedrek said. "But I'd still love it if you fed me."

"Yeah, of course. I feed everyone around here. Well, almost everyone. Certain people are too good for my food and only food touched by Sawyer's hand is good enough. Ridiculous."

Jedrek had no idea what she was talking about. All of the mates had raved about Viv at one time or another. Maybe the new fairy guy— Loch, Jedrek remembered his name after a minute— maybe it was him?

Viv huffed and began slinging food around. Jedrek leaned back against the wall and closed his eyes. The back door opened, and he glanced that way and smiled.

"Uncle Jed! What are you doing here?"

"Hey, Henry. Nick wanted to talk to Sawyer about some stuff, so I brought him over."

"Cool. So... what happened?"

Jedrek honestly didn't know what Nick wanted explained. "Long story, but she's gone. You don't have to worry about her anymore. We took her to the gates, and the goddess took care of her."

Henry gasped. "Seriously?"

"I promise. Nick was amazing."

"Uh-huh. I bet. So I hear he's your mate."

"Yeah."

"A lot of that going around these days."

There really was. First Meshaq. Then Solomon. Then him. He wondered who was next.

He leaned back again and listened as Henry babbled about things going on in their world. Nothing exciting, and nothing he hadn't already heard, but it was nice to get to sit and listen for a few. He hadn't had the opportunity in a long time to listen to one of Henry's spiels. Before he knew it, Viv had placed a heaping plate of food in front of him.

"Sawyer! Food!"

He heard feet trampling down the stairs and grinned when both Sawyer and Nick reappeared. Nick was waving what appeared to be a black credit card around with a grin.

"What's that?"

"We're being bank rolled. My brother's loaded."

"Bank rolled? For what?"

Sawyer's eyes widened and he turned to his brother. "You didn't tell him?"

"Not yet. I came to see you first. Wanted you to know I was okay. And now I need to eat. I'm starving."

The buzz of magic from the goddesses had started to wear off. Nick turned to the bowl of pasta Viv handed him like he'd not eaten in a week. He barely even chewed.

Jedrek ate his with a little more restraint, even as he watched the conversation Sawyer and Henry were having with their eyes. Apparently whatever news Nick had shared with his brother was big. Well, bigger than the fact that they were up against the god of air. That was a pretty significant bombshell. But that didn't seem to be the one that had Sawyer in a lather.

"Man, that was amazing. Viv, I have my brother's credit card. Can I steal you?"

"Honey, I have a card like that already. And I promise, you can't afford me. But I will feed you anytime you want."

"You know, my mate here can do the portal thing. What time's breakfast?"

Jedrek growled at him. "Nick."

"What? Fine. We need to go. Solomon and the others are waiting."

"Thanks for the food, Viv," Jedrek said.

"Yeah," Nick added. "You're my favorite, Viv. Seriously awesome. Thank you."

Nick dragged Jedrek back outside. "Home, Jeeves."

Jedrek pinched his ass and opened a portal. Maybe he'd finally find out what the hell was going on.

NICK

Nick's mind swirled and had since the goddess had spoken to him. He couldn't believe she had such faith in him. He went through the portal with Jedrek and waited in the stone circle for someone to come let them out. "What a night."

"And it's not over yet."

Nick looked up and wrapped his arms around Jedrek's waist. "You really trust me, don't you? Even though I was a crazed maniac when you first met me."

"You weren't that bad. Just a messed-up shifter. Dealing with that is sort of my job description. Besides, you're hot. I'm willing to forgive a lot for an ass like yours."

Nick snorted and pushed into his mate. "Things are going to get nuts in a few.

He wanted his scent on Jedrek. He needed to touch him.

"How so?"

Nick tucked his face into Jedrek's neck and breathed. "We've got to go rescue some kids."

Jedrek tensed and Nick raised his head. "Why are we waiting?"

"It's not time. The goddess told me to wait for a sign. She said I'd know."

"Well that's vaguely ominous."

"I thought so, too. But I don't know. It's like... I can almost feel her talking to me. Not talking, talking. But I don't know."

"Your instincts," Jedrek said. "My goddess can communicate with us that way."

"Oh. That makes sense. Sort of. As much as any of the rest of it does."

"Wait. When you said rescue kids..."

Nick grinned. "Congratulations. We're now alphas to a whole slew of shifter kids who've never known anything but captivity!"

Jedrek swayed for a minute but Nick held him steady. "I'm not an alpha."

"Yeah. What would you be though? What's Solomon's mate?"

"Alpha-mate."

"Yeah. That's you."

Jedrek stroked his back. "Solomon is still my alpha."

"Well, yeah. Course he is. You're a hellhound. But you're still my mate. Right?"

"Yeah."

"And you're part of my pack. I can't really explain it. It's like Solomon's your boss, but I'm your partner. Or something. We'll make it work." Nick tightened his hold on Jedrek. He didn't think he could let him go if he wanted to. Not now. Not when everything was going to change and Nick needed something to hold on to more than ever.

"Breathe, Nick."

Nick sucked in a breath and tucked his face back into Jedrek's neck. "I can't do this without you. Isn't that crazy?"

"Not crazy. But, um, how many kids are we talking here?"

Nick wasn't entirely sure.

"Is someone going to let us out of here already? Keziah!"

"Nick?"

"I don't know. But I'm getting worried. Why hasn't someone come? Can we get out of here?"

"Someone's coming."

Keziah came running toward them, and it took Nick a minute to process what he was seeing.

"Ollie's here," Jedrek announced.

"What...why... how..."

"Don't ask questions. But if Ollie says I have an idea, just say no."

Keziah was covered in some sort of body paint. He looked slightly frantic. "What the hell?"

"Ollie said he needed to practice and then he just... and I... there was... I don't know."

Nick grunted. "Let me out. I have things to do."

Keziah lowered the wards and led them into the gated area. Solomon sat on Zaire's porch with her. Ben was playing in front of the house with the cubs, but the moment they caught Nick's scent, they froze.

Lionel turned around and ran, and Ariella wasn't far behind him. Leandra came out of Izzy's house carrying a couple sippy cups, which she immediately fumbled. She managed not to drop them, and then she was running, too. The twins got to him first and Nick knelt down. They rubbed against him, and he returned the gesture. He needed them to smell like him. Anything else would make him crazy. Leandra dropped to her knees beside him and leaned in as well. Jedrek pressed against his back and Nick wanted to scream. So he did. He threw back his head but what emerged instead was a roar, one so loud it rattled the windows.

He had his pack.

"Gonna need you and the kids tonight," Nick said softly. "We have work to do."

"You seem different," Leandra said. "Stronger. How is this even possible? The lion... it was gone. You didn't smell like lion anymore. I don't understand."

"I guess the goddess had other plans for me," Nick explained. "Did you know that your lion is part of your soul? I didn't know that."

Leandra shrugged. "Seems as good an explanation as any."

"Are you like, Son of somebody? Or I guess daughter?"

"Xsayarsa," Jedrek supplied.

"Yeah, that."

Leandra's eyes widened. "Uh, no. Shit, Nick. Seriously? You're lucky you're mated or every female lion in a million-mile radius would be showing up here. Actually, you might get that anyway. Mated and not looking to knock them up? Yeah. I think a few will sign up for a ride on the Nick express."

Jedrek growled. Nick looked up at him. "As if."

"No lionesses. Only Leandra."

"Deal. Well, unless you say it's okay first. Because of the mission."

"Agreed."

"What mission?"

Jedrek stiffened against him and Nick looked up again.

"Not now." Jedrek was glaring at his arm.

Something in Nick solidified. A *knowing*.

"It's time."

"What?"

"What's the arm deal?" Nick asked.

"My sigil. It's how my goddess lets me know... oh. Shit."

"Yep. Looks like our first rescue mission starts now."

Jedrek glanced at the sigil once more then back down to Nick.

"Leave the portal open for me, *dear*."

Jedrek smirked. "Fine, *honey*. Going."

Solomon came down the porch and they walked toward the circle of rocks again. Keziah came back with Ollie in tow. He'd managed to wash the paint off. Ben and Zaire met them in the yard.

"Solomon said you needed us."

"Yeah. The goddess gave me a job, and I need your help."

"Wait? Seriously?" Ollie asked.

"Yes. You know we got Mrs. Foote, right?"

"Yeah, Uncle Sol told us."

"Well, the goddess convinced her to give up all her secrets, including where there were more kids like you."

Ben began to tremble, but Zaire and Keziah both surrounded him. Ollie's mouth tightened into a grim line. "What can we do?"

"I'm bringing them here. They're going to be safe, but I could really use a hand. I don't know shit about kids."

Ollie nodded and looked at his brother. "We can do this."

Ben nodded. "Of course."

"Good. I'll be back soon. Keziah, with me."

He glanced at Zaire, but she simply nodded.

Keziah followed him to the stone circle, where as promised, Jedrek had left the portal open. "You ready?"

"I hope so."

Nick grabbed the back of his neck and gave it a squeeze. "Kids are depending on us. You've got this. Focus. Breathe."

"I will."

Nick nodded once more. He stepped through the portal and immediately lost his mind. He smelled blood. Jedrek's blood. He shoved Keziah behind him, half shifted, and let out a roar. Everything froze. A man— some sort of witch probably— had his mate against the wall. Jedrek hadn't shifted, which meant he probably couldn't. Nick had no clue what was happening, but his mate was in danger. He leapt. The man spun and he had something glowing in his hand. Nick didn't care. He had the guy by the throat and ripped it out. Blood went everywhere, but particularly all over his mate.

His breath heaved. He looked up and Jedrek stared down at him. And there were the flame-filled eyes he loved.

"Where's your alpha?" Nick demanded.

Jedrek moved nothing but his eyes, which glanced down a hallway.

"What's wrong?"

"It's a spell," Keziah said. "I've got it. He'll be fine. Go help Solomon."

Nick turned to Keziah, who stepped back and lowered his eyes. "Sorry."

"For what?" Nick snapped.

"You're, ya know, freaking me out."

Nick scowled and turned to Jedrek. "Stay here. Keziah!"

"On it."

Nick gave Jedrek one last look. This time his mate's eyes had a bit of sparkle to them. His mate was amused. He'd show him amused. Later. He had a job to do.

He smelled the alpha down the hall. A door was barricaded shut. Nick banged on the door. "Solomon!"

"Here."

"Open the door."

Then Nick heard a whimper of pain. It wasn't Solomon.

Nick roared again. He slammed his fist into the door and something blew him back down the hall. He hit the ground and rolled finding his feet again moments later. Keziah came running. "What was that?"

"Ward."

"Shit, Nick. What'd you do to it?"

"Punched it."

Keziah looked at him like he was an idiot. "You really don't know shit about magic, do you?"

Nick growled. "Work on it. I've got your back. Where's Jedrek?"

"Guarding the door. He said for me to tell you that was hot."

"I said fucking hot!" Jedrek's voice came from the front of the house and Nick smiled.

Damn straight he was hot. "Gonna—"

"Nick! Little ears!" Keziah yelled.

Nick growled. "FINE. Gonna, you know, you later!"

"I know," Jedrek called. "Gonna, you know, you, too."

Nick grinned. Then turned back to the task at hand.

"Aren't you done yet?" Nick snapped.

Keziah raised his hands and stepped away. "There you go, mighty alpha hear you roar."

"Don't be such a smart ass."

"I can't help it. I take after my alpha."

It took a second for the words to process. Then Nick grinned. He grabbed Keziah by the neck again. "Damn straight you do. Let's do this."

"Door's stuck."

Nick scoffed. He poked the lion inside him, made sure he knew their alpha-hood was being challenged. The lion huffed, and puffed, and then he roared. The door opened. Nick turned back to Keziah, raised his hand to his mouth, and blew on his knuckles. "Easy, peasy."

"Uh..."

Nick glanced down the hall, where Solomon stood with his hand on the knob. *Oh.*

"Oh."

"But, you know, your roar is freaky as all get out. That's new. And this whole—" Keziah waved his hand around Nick's head.

"What?"

"Nick, your hair is crazy."

"It's a half-shift," Jedrek called from the front.

"So helpful, dear!" Nick yelled back.

"Hurry up, honey. I'm ready to go home and you know now."

Nick grinned.

Solomon had his face in his hand. "Dear Goddess, help me."

"Why are you just standing there?" Nick griped.

Solomon raised his head and scowled. "I think this is your job."

"Oh, right." Nick sauntered down the hall and past Solomon into the room. There were three kids huddled in the corner. They looked up at him and Nick wanted to go out and kill that asshole magic guy again. "You ready to get out of here?"

They looked fearful. Nick didn't blame them. He knelt down and held out his arms. "Come on. I'm hungry. And I really need a nap."

He was hit by three bodies a second later, each of them clinging to him. Nick pulled in a breath and let out a rumbling purr. He looked down, startled at the sound.

"That's new," Solomon said.

Nick scowled at him, even as he pushed to his feet. These ones were all little, somewhere between Sophie-size and the twins size.

"Hide your faces," Nick said. "Close your eyes, okay?"

Three nods against his chest.

He carried them into the hall, and Keziah paled.

"Come on. Let's get them home. Hey, do we have any cheeseburgers? Man, I could really go for a burger."

Solomon stepped up beside him, as they walked toward Jedrek and the door. "I have a connection. How do you feel about chimichangas?"

"I feel hungry, Solomon."

"We just ate," Jedrek said.

"And?"

Jedrek shrugged and opened a portal. "I could eat."

Nick carried the kids through, and Keziah dropped the wards once they were all through and the portal closed again. Nick took them to where the others waited. The kids were still up— way past their bedtime and he was not taking the blame for that no matter how much Izzy glared at him.

The twins were shifted and Sophie was running around with them like a little crazy person. "Hey, little monsters. I made some new friends."

"Nick! We want to play with Simba!"

"Simba?" One of the heads against his chest poked up.

Nick groaned. "Fine. I'll shift. But only if you stop calling me Simba!"

The kids in his arms raised their heads, watching eagerly.

"You guys wanna shift, too?" They looked suspicious. "You can if you want. But if you want me to shift, I have to put you down. I kinda need all my arms and legs, you know?"

"That's good," Ben rumbled quietly. "If we know what they are, we can help them better. Remember how Nana made sure I had fruit?"

Ollie nodded. "Still does. Blueberry fiend."

"Blueberry?" One of the kids perked up at that.

Ben grinned.

Nick knelt down and sat them down. He leaned his head against each of theirs in turn, then opened his arms. All three of them were wearing not much more than oversized T-shirts, so when they stripped and changed, Nick was met with a couple surprises. One, in the form of two tiny tigers. His breath caught. But the other, was a blur of dark fur. A long fluffy tail wrapped around his neck, and what felt like fingers gripped his hair.

Ollie's mouth fell open. Ben looked stunned.

"Uh, guys?"

"Is that a marmoset?" Ben gasped.

"What's a marmoset?" Nick grumbled.

"A kind of monkey."

Said monkey leapt off of Nick's head and landed on Ollie. It wrapped around him and began to pluck at the rainbow-striped streaks in Ollie's hair.

The little tigers chuffed at him, so Nick stripped and changed, letting out another of his roars. All the kids ran to him, and he made sure he marked them all as his. His chest puffed out. He shook out his mane. And then he ran. Not too fast, because there were a lot of little legs and he wasn't that much of a jerk. His mate joined him, running by his side. Leandra caught up a minute later. Even Solomon joined in. Ollie ran along, too, still in his human form and with their new monkey shifter on his head. They darted down the street to the gate, then turned around and walked back.

Nick couldn't help feeling proud of what they'd done. If this was his mission, it was a good one. He could get behind this. He had purpose. But man, he really needed a nap.

Nick woke up in his favorite position. Jedrek was sprawled out on their bed, and Nick was using him as his personal body pillow. He tucked his face back into Jedrek's neck and breathed. And choked. Not that Jedrek didn't smell amazing. He did. But he also stunk. They probably should have taken the time to shower after the whole bloody witch guy thing, but Nick hadn't had the patience. By the time they got the kids fed and settled in a giant sleepover on Izzy's living room floor, Nick had wanted nothing more than to you know his mate. And they'd you knowed multiple times before they passed out in exhaustion.

Now, though, the cloying scent of other swarmed Nick's nose. He didn't like it. He poked Jedrek in the side. "Again?" Jedrek groaned.

"Was that a complaint"

Jedrek snorted. "No. What's wrong?"

"You smell weird. Come shower."

"What?"

"You smell like that witch guy's blood."

Jedrek groaned. "You're just noticing this now?"

"Yeah? So?"

"We're going to have to change the sheets then."

"Yeah? So?" Nick poked him again. "Come on. It's grossing me out."

Jedrek rolled over and glared. "You fucked me unconscious and now—" he turned his head and glanced at the clock, "—less than three hours later, you wake me up and want me to shower?"

"Yeah? So?"

Jedrek huffed. "Fine, but if you wake me up again after this, we're going to have words."

"Nah. I'll just fuck you unconscious again. I don't mind. It'll be fine."

That got him a smile.

Jedrek wandered into the bathroom while Nick took the sheets off the bed. He took them outside and dumped them off the side of the porch. He went back inside, then realized he didn't know if they had any other sheets. Oh well. He'd slept on worse. He'd just pull the blanket up. Not like they needed one anyway. Jedrek kept him warm enough.

He went into the bathroom where his mate was already under the steaming water. He had his head tipped back, water pouring over the mohawk, pulling it to a point on his shoulders. It pointed due south. To one of Nick's all-time favorite spots. Damn, Jedrek was so gorgeous. He could write an ode to his ass. If he had a clue how to write an ode. But he could probably figure it out.

But now, he wanted to not be outside the shower anymore. He opened the door and stepped in.

Jedrek lifted his head and wiped the water out of his face.

"Fuck, you're gorgeous."

"Yeah?"

"Don't be dumb. You know you are. Why can't I keep my hands off you?"

Jedrek shrugged. "Like I care."

Water dripped over Jedrek's chest, down his body. His cock was just right there, water pouring off of it. And suddenly, Nick was very, very thirsty. He dropped so his knees and ran his hands down Jedrek's thighs. "So fucking perfect."

He didn't give Jedrek a chance to argue with him. He sucked the tip of his dick into his mouth, swirled his tongue around the ridge, then gave it a nice, hard suck for good measure.

Jedrek groaned and moved his legs apart a little further. Nick wrapped his fist around the base, pulling and stroking, even as it grew harder in his hand. He continued working the tip, knowing exactly what drove Jedrek over the edge. He raised his other hand, teased his balls, gripped them in his hand, rolled them. Jedrek's legs trembled.

His mate began to move his hips, chasing the release Nick had so expertly built. He gave his balls a tug, felt them tightening his hold, and sucked harder on the tip. Jedrek groaned, spurting his release into Nick's mouth. He eagerly drank it down, and a purr began in his chest.

"Oh fuck," Jedrek yelled. "Fuck. Fuck."

He came harder, and Nick focused on getting it all. *His.* Jedrek was his. No one else ever got this.

When he released Jedrek from his hold and looked up, Jedrek stared at him with hungry eyes. He pushed to his feet, his cock sticking out proudly. Jedrek eyed it and licked his lips. Then he groaned.

And looked at his arm in dismay.

"Are you kidding me?" Nick snarled.

Jedrek turned off the water and jumped out of the shower, snagging a towel as he ran back into the bedroom. Nick leaned against the tiled wall and scowled. He shook his fist at the ceiling. "I know you did this on purpose."

He swore heard the goddess's tinkling laughter in reply. He gave his dick one last sad look before climbing out of the shower and shifting into his lion form. He wasn't in the mood to get dressed. Fuck pants. Fuck them hard. He wanted to roar his displeasure, but he'd already gotten in trouble for that once in the form of a scathing text message from Izzy that said if he couldn't come quietly, he didn't get to come at all because she'd drop off all six kids in his living room and let him deal with them. Needless to say, he'd come quietly the next time. And the time after that.

Jedrek appeared fully dressed in the doorway and grinned down at him. "Time to go to work."

EPILOGUE
JEDRICK

Nick stormed into the bar and stomped immediately to the back where Jedrek sat on a stool, performing his duty as bouncer for the bar. Jedrek couldn't stop his grin if he tried, even if Nick looked like he wanted to disembowel someone.

"Do I look like an idiot to you?" Nick demanded.

Jedrek wisely kept his mouth shut. Instead, he reached for his mate's hips and pulled him between his thighs. Nick's eyes flared the beautiful golden yellow Jedrek loved so much.

"Do people think I'm stupid? I will cut a bitch."

Jedrek couldn't help it. He laughed.

Nick growled.

"Oh, come on, love. You can't expect me not to laugh at that."

"Yeah. Maybe. And don't think I don't know that you decided to take this shift at the bar on purpose."

They both knew he had, so Jedrek didn't bother trying to deny it. It wasn't that he didn't want to help; he did. But damn, the idiots coming out of the woodwork were enough to make him crazy.

"You ever see that movie *Annie*?" Nick asked.

"Can't say that I have."

"I can, unfortunately, say I've watched it like a hundred times. Not because I wanted to, but because it was Mama Thea's favorite. And, I will tell you that I loved that woman. You know I did."

"I know," Jedrek said.

"But she couldn't carry a tune in a bucket. And she'd sing that *Tomorrow* song at the top of her lungs and it was *torture*."

"I believe you."

"Sometimes, I think she did it to make me crazy. But when Sawyer was little, he loved it, too. So he'd want to watch it with her, and he wouldn't watch it without me and Mikey. He was such a brat."

"He loved his big brothers. Still does."

"Whatever. Anyway, there was this scene where the rich guy offers up this huge prize for Annie's real parents and all these scumbags line up and are basically asking for a handout. They don't care about Annie. They just want the money. That's what I'm dealing with, Jed. Scum bags. Asshole scum bags who think I'm an idiot."

They'd spread the word that they had cubs in need of parents. There were too many of them to handle on their own, and Nick hadn't really wanted to have them in one big place like an orphanage, even though that option had been on the table. No, he'd wanted them to have parents, like he'd had with Mama Thea and Papa Smith. Like Ben and the others had with Vaughn and Sam.

Problem was, finding people Nick liked enough to let them actually live in the compound with the coven, because Nick had claimed them all as his pack, and he wasn't letting then live anywhere else. To say that Nick was overprotective was an understatement. He'd become almost as bad as Zaire. Jedrek loved it.

"What can I do?"

"Nothing. Keziah wants to tweak the wards a bit and only let people with good intentions in. Course, I told him that might be a problem, because whenever you're around, I *never* have good intentions."

"Oh, I don't know. I'd say your intentions are very, very good. Fantastic, even. In fact—"

"No, don't distract me. Wait. Scratch that. Distract me a little."

"Don't even think about it," Walt barked from the kitchen window.

Nick turned and glared. "Walt! I have *needs*."

"Yeah, well, I have eyes. Go fuck somewhere else. I'm making you nachos."

"Oh, I'll wait to fuck then."

Jedrek grunted. "Hey."

"Walt's *nachos*, Jed. What do you expect me to do?"

Walt's nachos were a thing of beauty. Everybody with half a brain knew it. And all they had left in the freezer was a weird casserole with asparagus in it that neither of them were willing to try. Nick would probably call Viv again and bat his eyes at her or something. He always managed to get them a fridge full of food that they didn't have to cook.

"So did you find anybody decent?"

"Yeah. I'm going to ask Solomon to grill them, though. Literally. Flamey eyes and all hellhound alpha scary. That ought to weed out the last of 'em. Plus, I'll gut anyone who does wrong by my kids."

His kids. Jedrek tugged him closer. Goddess, it was hot when Nick got all growly and protective.

"How's construction coming along?"

His mate had also had a meeting that morning with his brother's mate, Eduard. Sawyer apparently had more money than... well, Jedrek would say God, but since Sawyer was one, that kind of lost its effect. Sawyer had more money than he knew what to do with, though, so he was basically funding the entire venture. Which was good. Because they now had a couple dozen mouths to feed.

"Fine. Eduard got the permits pushed through. They're getting the fence put up first. No way am I not having a fence. And he found a contractor who was in between building subdivisions so they're going to put up ours fast. There were a lot of zeros on the end of that check. A whole lot of zeros."

"Glad Sawyer was able to help."

"Yeah. He's good at this shit. I'm just glad Eduard was able to get the land all around us. Zaire had tried, but Eduard's bank account is a whole lot bigger than hers."

Jedrek was well aware. He had a griffin managing his money, too. Not that he had as much of it as Sawyer or Eduard, but Nick would probably be surprised. The goddess made sure her champions were well provided for, and Meshaq had taught them early on to let the griffins handle it. What else was Jedrek going to do with a pile of cash? He'd insisted on paying for his and Nick's place, though, and had secretly put in a call to Eduard for a favor of his own. It was a surprise for his mate. No cookie cutter monstrosity for them. He couldn't wait for the final plans to be finished so he could show Nick.

"And he really got everything approved already? That's incredible."

"Eduard doesn't mess around. I guess he's going to send one of his cousins to help manage everything and keep the contractor on his toes. I don't know. I just sit there and scowl and he does the rest. Sawyer wants to put in a community pool. He says the kids need a pool.

"Some of 'em, maybe. Calder's been letting them play in the stream."

"Yeah. But a *pool*. They're dangerous."

Jedrek grinned and tucked his face into Nick's neck. "We'll put a big fence around it. And a ward."

"Oh, that's a good idea," Nick rumbled. "And I guess Sawyer and Henry spent a bunch of time researching playgrounds and stuff and came up with some plan. Did you know we've apparently made playgrounds too safe? There's a whole thing about it. I didn't understand shit about what they were explaining, but it's a thing."

"Kids wanna be wild and free. Test their boundaries. I get that. We all survived."

"Yeah," Nick said. He kissed Jedrek's neck, then inhaled, before making a whimpering whining sound. "How much longer for those nachos?"

Jedrek chuckled and nipped at Nick's throat. "Soon."

"Good. Because I'm cranky. Next time, you have to stay with me."

Jedrek didn't protest. He'd find a way to get out of the meetings again. Nick knew it. He knew it. There was no use pretending otherwise.

"Sam said I have to make a decision about school."

"School?"

"Yeah. He said the kids need to go to school. And that decision was best left to their alpha."

"That'd be you," Jedrek grumbled.

"Tell me about it. But like I know shit about schools."

Nick used that excuse a lot. Claimed he didn't know. And maybe he didn't. What Nick did have was finely tuned instincts. He may not know, but he could make a decision. It was crazy watching him maneuver through this new challenge. Jedrek loved seeing him in action. And the kids absolutely loved him. Jedrek had never seen anything like it, and he'd seen the total adoration Ben and the others had given to Vaughn and Sam. This was different. Nick was their hero, their savior. He wasn't going to be their dad, though. He was their alpha. Jedrek hadn't really considered the difference until he'd seen Nick with them.

He played with them, trained with them, comforted them, and kept them all in line. He treated them like packmates, equals. He listened, even to the smallest of the cubs, and if what they said made sense, Nick agreed. If he didn't, he told them no, and why. None of them had that before. Quite a few of them hadn't gotten up the nerve to try to negotiate, but the longer they spent in his company, the braver they became.

And then there were the naps. Epic naps which Jedrek had come to think of as puppy piles. Nick had cleared out the dining room of their house—like they ever used the table to eat anyway, and it really did get great afternoon sun—and he'd put in a bunch of pillows and soft blankets. Every afternoon, he'd give a giant roar. It had come to be known as the nap bell. After he roared, Nick would wander into the dining room, find himself a sunny spot, and lay down. He'd be snoring within seconds. And then the horde would come, tiptoeing the first days, then stampeding as they grew more confident. Nick ended up with the majority of the kids piled on and around him, sleeping away the last tendrils of the physical trauma they'd endured.

Well, most of them, anyway. One of the kids had stolen Jedrek's heart. They still hadn't figured out exactly what she was. They'd done everything short of take her directly to the goddess and didn't have an answer. But Jedrek didn't care. She wasn't well, that much he knew for certain. He'd taken to calling her Robin, because she had the prettiest blue eyes. She even had wings, even though they didn't work. They seemed to hurt her, and she had trouble walking sometimes. Jedrek had her on his shoulders more often than not, and Vaughn was already working on a way to help. It just made Jedrek want to hunt them all down again, demand answers, and then send them back to hell after he'd made sure they had enough punishment here.

He tried not to think about what would happen when Nick found parents for her. When it wasn't him carrying her on his shoulders anymore.

"You're breaking my heart," Nick grumbled. "Cut it out already."

"What?"

"Like I don't know? Are we back to me being an idiot again?"

"Order up!"

Walt's yell from the window didn't even distract Nick from his glare. He stared Jedrek down, forcing him to hold his gaze. "I think I'm the idiot."

"That's what I've been saying. No one will believe me. Here's the thing. I know what you want. I know you wanna keep her, but Jed, if we do that, we gotta do it right. I don't know shit about kids, and they're a lot of work. I mean, I was talking to Sam about all the things

I've gotta keep up with as their alpha. He made me a spreadsheet. With tabs. And links. I'm more scared of that spreadsheet than I am of the goddess herself."

"Yeah, I know." It broke his heart to admit it, but he didn't know anything about kids anyway, and his life was too crazy to even think about bringing a kid into it. It was dumb. He'd just be her favorite uncle or something, just like he did with Sam and Vaughn's kids, like he did with Sophie.

A sudden sharp pain on his ass startled him out of his thoughts. His mate had pinched him. Hard. "Ow. What the fuck, Nick?"

"One, go get my nachos for me. I'm fading away to nothing, here. Two. We're keeping Robin. Shut up. No one can love her more than you do. Like I'm letting her go to some idiot when she can have the best dad on the planet. Okay, second best. No third. I mean, I love you, Jed, you know I do, but dude, Sam and Vaughn are impressive."

"I'll take third place to them."

"I figured. But we're gonna have to learn to cook."

Nick's stomach chose that moment to rumble and he stared down at it. Jedrek pushed him aside and toward the empty booth at the back. He went to the window and lifted the plate of nachos. Walt stuck his head around the corner and glared. "What's that face?"

"I'm gonna be a dad."

Jedrek grinned, ignoring the clatter as Walt dropped something in the kitchen. He took the plate to the booth and slid in beside Nick. "I'm gonna get Vaughn to give me lessons, or whatever. And I'll read the spreadsheet. We can do this."

"Yeah." Nick leaned against him and scooped up one of the overloaded chips. "I can't wait to tell Sawyer and Mikey they're going to be uncles."

Jedrek grinned and looked around the bar. His pack hadn't changed, only grown. And even though there were still uncertain times ahead. Even though they didn't know what was coming or from what direction, Jedrek didn't care. He'd found what he needed in the eye of this storm, and he'd give anyone hell who tried to take it from him.

———

WANT MORE of Nick and his pack of orphans? Check out All Kidding Aside, Magical Mates Book One.

OR TURN the page to find out what happens when Achim meets the Prince of Hell...and finds out Ozias is his mate in Hell Breaks Loose.

PREVIEW: HELL BREAKS LOOSE

"I need four drafts, three single-shot whiskeys, six snakebites, and a strawberry daiquiri." Shelly unloaded empty glasses from her tray as she rattled off her drink orders to Achim.

She was their best waitress for a reason. No way could Achim have remembered that many orders without writing them all down.

Achim pulled the handle of the beer tap, filling a glass somewhat expertly. It required his full and complete attention. Cody, Hair of the Dog's actual bartender and the alpha-mate of the hellhound pack, stood at the other end of the polished wooden bar, expertly making cocktails while charming all the customers who had the pleasure of watching him work.

"Say again?" Achim asked, realizing suddenly that Shelly expected him to make the drinks she'd requested.

Shelly scowled. "Why do they put you behind the bar? You're worse than Meshaq ever was."

Achim shrugged and focused on the glass in his hand. Cody would be annoyed if he got too much foam on the top. "Could be worse. Want me to get Solomon?"

With a huff, she rounded the bar and rattled off the list to Cody.

Achim grinned and returned his attention to the mug in his hand. Shelly knew as well as he did that their current alpha was a much larger disaster behind the bar than their former alpha ever had been, especially because it pushed Solomon over the edge when customers flirted with his mate.

"Four more," Cody said to Achim as he slid down the bar and began filling the blender with ice.

"I'm on it."

Cody laughed and took the one glass he'd managed to fill. "Nice job."

"You make it look easy."

"It is easy. You just have to be patient."

And there was the rub.

Patient wasn't a word anyone would use to describe Achim, especially not lately. With so much change going on in their world, his hellhound couldn't seem to settle. Or maybe it was his human side. Achim honestly wasn't sure. All he knew was he felt a bone-deep level of exhaustion. His entire pack did. They'd been run ragged the past few months with all the magic problems occurring in their realm.

He wouldn't let his alpha-mate down, though. For Cody to ask for help behind the bar meant he was desperate. He normally didn't like any of them working with him because it messed with his vibe.

Whatever that meant.

Achim grabbed another pint glass and held it beneath the tap. He tugged the lever once again, releasing another stream of the deep amber brew into the glass. Cody had chosen the variety himself from one of their local breweries. The customers seemed to love it.

Personally, Achim thought beer tasted like warm piss. Give him a whiskey any day of the week, not that alcohol did a lot for him. No, being a champion of a Goddess had a lot of perks. It also had a few downsides. Getting a buzz from booze wasn't really in the cards.

With another nicely filled mug in hand, Achim turned to show off his mad skills to Cody, hoping to get another smile from his alpha-mate. His sigil activated at the same time, and searing pain shot up his arm. The handle slipped from his hand as his arm spasmed, and the mug shattered when it hit the ground.

Silence filled the bar.

All eyes were on him.

Achim fought to maintain control as the burning pain worsened.

"Oops, my bad," Cody said loudly and with a laugh. "That's what I get for letting these lugs help, isn't it, boys?"

The regulars cackled, used to Cody's teasing them about everyone else's general lack of skill behind the bar. Cody mumbled under his breath, low enough that only his pack's enhanced hearing would pick up the words. "Vice, here now."

"I've got to go," Achim said. He clenched his arm as he stepped over the glass and spreading puddle of beer. "Sorry for the mess."

"What's wrong?" Cody asked, keeping his voice quiet even as he blocked Achim's path. His gaze drifted down to Achim's arm, which he still held tight.

"I don't know. I'm being called, though."

The sigil meant the Goddess had a task for him, and it wasn't something he could ignore. Even if her mark had never hurt before when she called him.

Vice hurried toward them from his position standing guard at the back of the bar. "What's wrong?"

"The sigil doesn't hurt, does it?" Cody hissed the question, never taking his eyes off Achim.

"No," Vice said. "Of course not. The Goddess wouldn't—"

"Yeah, that's what I thought, but it's hurting Achim."

His packmates shared a glance. Cody returned his attention to Achim, his brows settling into an impressive glare.

"I'm fine," Achim said. He released his hold on the sigil and ignored the searing pain. "I've got to go."

Cody and Vice followed him as he hurried out of the bar into the chill winter air. Cody shivered, and Vice slipped off his leather jacket and handed it to him. Achim hadn't bothered wearing a jacket. Unless the temperatures were downright frigid, they hampered his ability to fight. Plus, unlike Vice, he'd never been able to pull off the black-leather look. He always seemed like the guy who'd stolen his big brother's jacket, even though he was one of the bigger members of his pack.

As a human, though, Cody did get cold. He glared at Achim, even as he slid his arms into the sleeves of the jacket and pulled it around him. He continued to follow Achim as he tried to find a place to open his portal.

The parking lot was too bright, with the huge floodlights Sol had installed a while back for safety. They made it so Achim had to go to the other side of the building to find a place away from any unsuspecting human eyes.

"Achim, please wait for Sol," Cody said. He sounded scared, and Achim's beast stirred. None of them liked it when Cody was upset.

The sigil burned sharply once more, and Achim couldn't hide his wince. "That's not how this works, Cody, and you know it. I'll be back soon."

He opened the portal, but instead of the floating red-and-orange circular flames that always appeared, it was an eerie icy blue.

"No fucking way," Cody said. "You are *not* going in there. Not without Solomon or another member of the pack. Forget it."

"Sol's on a mission of his own," Achim replied. "And the Goddess called me. Keep a close eye on him." The last part Achim directed to his packmate, who stared at him with his forehead creased with concern.

Vice nodded. "Caution."

Achim returned the nod before glancing at the unusual flames once more. Without another thought, he stepped through the portal and into a completely unfamiliar landscape. The portal closed behind him, separating him from his pack.

It shouldn't have felt so final.

He shivered as he took in the view. In all his years as a hellhound, Achim had seen most of the human realm and quite a few others as well.

He'd never seen this before.

A barren, frozen landscape lay before him on one side, but on the other, a lush green forest beckoned. The problem with said beckoning forest was it sent a shiver of dread down his spine.

His instincts had spoken, loud and clear. He wasn't to go near...

Before he could process further, a figure ran from between the trees, heading directly for him. A black cloak billowed around their body, floating almost unnaturally in the stillness of the frigid air.

Achim heard shouted words from a deep masculine voice, but in another first, he couldn't understand a word the man said. He could understand all spoken languages. It was part of the hellhound gift. The Goddess made it so they could communicate with anyone, anywhere.

It took another moment for him to realize the man wasn't the only thing in the woods. Hellhounds came out next, following the man—no, not following. *Chasing.*

Achim ran toward the danger, ready to help his fellow hellhounds apprehend whatever creature they chased. He'd learned in his many years as a champion that human-shaped creatures were often the vilest of all.

"For the love of Aeshma's asshole, get the fuck out of here!"

With a crackling of static, the man's voice suddenly translated itself. Achim prepared to shift... and couldn't. His beast prowled inside him, ready to attack, but for the first time since he'd become a hellhound, it didn't answer his call.

The man raised what looked like a giant gnarled stick and waved it around. The hellhounds howled and... got distracted? Ice flew around them, pelting them and providing enough of an obstruction to keep them from gaining ground on their target.

Achim kept his eyes on their prey, determined to help his brethren even as he tried to figure out what the hell was happening. It took him entirely too long to process, even as the creatures chasing the man tumbled into a pile and began attacking one another.

These weren't hellhounds. Well, they were hellhounds. But not like him. No, they weren't *shifters*. These were the original beasts... the beasts before they merged with their human counterpart to become the guardians of the human realm.

Which meant—

"Oh fuck." Achim spun on his heel and ran, just as the man caught up with him.

He caught a glimpse of pink cheeks and full lips before the cloak hid the man's face once more. He wanted another look but realized the hellhounds weren't fighting one another anymore.

No, the distraction had only worked for a few seconds, and they were on the hunt again. No way in hell could they outrun the beasts. Achim knew exactly how fast they were since one resided inside him. He'd run as his hellhound many, many times, and his speed as a human was no match for his shifted form.

He scanned the landscape, hoping for some miracle. He even tried to activate the sigil on his arm, but nothing. Not even a tickle of awareness appeared, when the magic of the Goddess normally rushed to his defense. It didn't surprise him. If his beast couldn't respond to his call to shift, he doubted his ability to call a portal would be available to him.

Whatever this place was, he was stranded without his beast or his Goddess's magic. He was cut off from his Goddess and his pack. Achim fought the urge to throw back his head and howl.

"There! Go!"

The cloaked man pointed, and they rushed toward a large, jagged cliff at the edge of the freaky forest. Achim didn't question the strangeness of the landscape, as he could practically feel demon-dog breath on his neck.

The man scrambled up the cliff, nimble and fast. Achim attempted to follow, but his body was too bulky to gracefully climb. He managed to get out of range of the first snap of the hellhound's jaws, but it was close enough to feel the terrifying huff of hot breath on his ankle.

Achim gripped the stone cliff face in front of him and tried to move faster.

"Hurry up!"

Achim glanced up. The man had already reached a small ledge. He knelt on it, his hand reaching out. Achim grabbed it the moment he could, and with a strength that seemed unnatural, even under the circumstances, the man pulled Achim up beside him.

The hellhounds leaped and snarled beneath them, unable to climb the almost sheer rock face.

"What the hell...?"

The man blinked at him. "Who are you?"

"Achim."

The man inhaled, then scrunched up his nose like he'd caught the scent of something fouler than the hellhounds beneath them. "*Human.*"

Then he launched into a steaming rant that Achim once again couldn't translate. Not that he needed the words to understand the tone.

"Who are you?" Achim asked when the guy paused to take a breath.

It earned him a disdain-filled look he'd only seen the likes of once before... when he'd met the prince of the fae realm.

"I am Ozias, Prince of Hell. And you're not supposed to be here."

Read the rest of Achim and Ozias's story here in Hell Breaks Loose.

WANT MORE?

Join Macy's Moonlighters to stay up to date on the latest news and releases from Macy and find other readers to talk to about Macy's books.
http://readerlinks.com/l/1828821

Keep in touch with Macy Blake!
Join Macy's newsletter
http://readerlinks.com/l/1633213

ABOUT THE AUTHOR

Macy Blake believes in unicorns and fairies, in moonbeams and stardust, and that happily ever after comes in all colors of the rainbow. She loves to lose herself in paranormal romance, living vicariously through her favorite sexy fictional heroes. These days you can often find her lost in her imagination, trying to capture the magic of her own worlds. When she's not writing, she's busy arguing with her feisty German Shepherd, Minerva, and attempting to train her adorable pound puppies, Pomona and Severus.

Visit Macy's website
www.macyblake.com

Join Macy's newsletter
http://readerlinks.com/l/1633213

Macy's Moonlighters Facebook Group
http://readerlinks.com/l/1828821

patreon.com/MacyBlake

facebook.com/macy.blake.1042

instagram.com/authormacyblake

amazon.com/author/macyblake

bookbub.com/authors/macy-blake

ALSO BY MACY BLAKE

THE CHOSEN UNIVERSE

The Chosen Universe Box Sets

Read the Chosen Universe in chronological order.

The Chosen One

The mythical Chosen One is set to return with his eight guardians and correct the magical wrongs done centuries before.

Hellhound Champions

As the champions of the fire goddess, the hellhounds have one task: keep the secret of the supernatural world safe.

Magical Mates

After the Chosen One returns, magic is in the air, and shifters are finally finding their fated mates... with a little help on the side.

Chosen Champions

With magic in the human realm going haywire, a new group of Champions is called in to help keep the world safe.

Cosmo and the King

Cosmo never told any of his friends in the human realm that he ran away on his wedding day, leaving his king at the alter. Now Silenus has to track down Cosmo and convince him that they are meant for each other, even though his stubborn fiancé seems determined to challenge him at every turn.

Christmas Sprites

With magic in the human realm on the fritz, four Christmas Sprites find themselves trying to keep the Christmas spirit alive in Mistletoe Falls...and finding love along the way.

OTHER SERIES AND STAND ALONES

Shifter Scoundrels Series

Co-written with Charlie Cochet

An exciting new shifter series filled with shifter royalty, dashing heroes, spies, grand balls, gossip, and fashion. It's an exciting adventure filled with mystery, intrigue, and of course, romance.

Triad of Magic

Magical species should never mix...but when a mage and alpha werewolf find themselves bound together, their forbidden attraction becomes a magic all of its own.

Stand Alones

Diagnosis Wolf

Born This Way

DID YOU KNOW?

If you own a book or borrow it through Kindle Unlimited, you can get Whispersynced audiobooks at a discounted price.

The Chosen One • Hellhound Champions

Magical Mates • Chosen Champions

Shifter Scoundrels

Made in the USA
Las Vegas, NV
12 November 2023

80730228R00135